Behind a Painted Smile

Phoebe Neve

PublishNation, London

www.publishnation.co.uk

Thank you to my family and friends for the constant support and encouragement I received throughout.

Chapter 1

Wednesday 6th October 1971

The man walked across his living room floor towards the window.

His heart raced as he drew together the curtains - shutting out the outside world.

In the solitude and tranquillity of his home he could forget everything - concentrate solely on satisfying the lust that burned within him; a yearning that never diminished. And for the next few minutes he can once again enjoy his ultimate fantasy.

The bulge in his trousers was obvious now that his penis was swollen to full capacity. In just a few minutes he knows he will be able to free his throbbing manhood and pleasure himself.

He turns his attention to an old cine projector mounted on a tripod in the corner of the room and his hands shake when he winds a a reel of film onto the spool. He struggles to control the urge to slide a hand inside his trousers and bring himself an immediate orgasmic release. He stops what he`s doing for a moment and takes a deep breath to regain a modicum of control. *I must be patient*, he tells himself ... *only a few minutes longer now....*

Flickering images begin to appear on the white screen hanging in the alcove. His ritual begins.

Sprawling his body across his old worn sofa he hastily unzips his trousers and wraps his hand firmly around his throbbing bulge and starts his gentle stroking movements that will bring him to a climax.

Transfixed at the familiar sight of a naked man straddling a female body, who`s face is obscured, his stroking actions grow faster and harder. His fingers tighten around his throbbing penis as the scenario is played out on the screen. Though there is no sound he can imagine the whimpering moans of the female being eagerly fondled. The male shifts position and thrusts hard and fast into the female. The voyeur can hold back no longer. On the flickering screen the male withdraws his engorged penis and ejaculates over the pale skin of the naked female's belly.

Using his hand he squeezes every last drop from his loins. Gratified, the voyeur now turns his attention away from the images on the screen and looks down at his clenched fist dripping with his own warm juices. Yet again he has enjoyed the thrill of having a simultaneous orgasm with the male in the flickering film. It never fails to give him satisfaction.

On the screen appears the image of a young girl sat upright on a rug with tears trickling down her distraught face. Her arms wrapped around her naked body trying hopelessly to cover her small developing breasts.

He stares at the child's face displayed before him and smiles as he feels the familiar stirrings in his loins once again. One day soon he hopes to turn his fantasy into reality.

One day very soon...

Chapter 2

"Hello playmates," was the familiar greeting June Cowburn always had for her colleagues and that fateful day was no exception. Even on Monday mornings she was always happy and cheerful, bringing a smile to the faces of her workmates and residents.

June worked at Field Hall Residential Care Home. This was one of the better establishments for the care of the elderly in the small northern town of Burtley. During her ten years of working there she had become one of the most experienced members of staff. With her cheery disposition and a great rapport with most of the patients she was well respected by her workmates. If any of the old folk in her care looked to be having a bad day she always made it her aim to bring a smile to their tired and often lifeless faces.

As for residential care, Field Hall was a little on the small side with only a maximum of thirty five residents but it was one of the friendlier ones to work in and reside in. The old manor house was situated in Highfield Road, only a couple of minutes walking distance away from Burtley`s town centre. It had been well maintained over the years with a view from the front gates that was impressive and a most welcoming sight. A neat gravel drive and path lead up from the wrought iron front gates right up to the large front door. Well tendered gardens bordered the building with an array of shrubbery and plants adding a touch of colour throughout the changing seasons.

Attached to the back of the old property a large extension had been built on. This offered plenty of space for resident`s rooms, a spacious kitchen and a laundry area. The rooms, set in three corridors, were all the same size and decorated to the same high standard.

The inside of the manor house had been equally as tastefully decorated with a warm and welcoming feel about it. Often the smell of stale urine was noticeable in such establishments, but Field Hall always had the fragrance of fresh flowers to welcome visitors or prospective residents. It was a peaceful and happy place to work and June had come to think of it as her second home.

Being a care worker had become a most important part of June's life since her pathetic attempt at marriage had come to an abrupt end over a decade earlier. Divorce had left her needing to find a job and support herself. Her previous career as a bank clerk was a definite no go in June's opinion. It would have been a constant reminder of too many bad memories.

With vacancies for staff in local care homes she had been able to gain employment quite easily. Looking after the frail and elderly was not a job suited to everyone but it suited June. While she was busy caring for others she could put her own problems to the back of her mind. For most of the time it worked. But when she closed the door of her small flat at the end of a shift the happy smiling face would often quickly disappear.

Having a regular salary had meant June could afford to rent a nice flat in Chevins Road, one of the nicer residential parts of Burtley. Living alone suited her just fine and the outings with friends she had made during her years at Field Hall gave her a decent social life. She had not wanted or needed any male companions since setting up home as a single woman again and that was the way she intended it to stay. June was used to being alone. She had been alone for most of her fifty one years.

When living with her parents and later with husband Nigel, she had rarely been alone in the physical sense, but never had a confidante to turn to when she really needed help.

Chapter 3

June`s parents had been married almost sixteen years when she arrived on the scene. A baby had come as a complete surprise to Gwen and Herbert Sweet after years of trying for a family. They had been overjoyed when their bouncing baby girl made her entrance into the world on June 26th 1960. She was born in June and aptly named after the month. Herbert and Gwen both knew she would probably be their only child and so she was to become their cherished pride and joy.

Being an older first time mother had made Gwen overly *Somewhat* protective. Thinking she had June`s best interests at heart, her mother had tried to shelter her from the nasty and seedier aspects of life. And what a good job of it she had done.

Gwen had one brother, Denis, who had never married. He had always said that he loved his young niece as if she were his own flesh and blood. June grew up in a close knit family and loved having her Uncle Denis around. She had one aunt, an uncle and cousin from her father`s side of the family, who she rarely saw.

Early memories of her favourite uncle were happy ones. He was about five feet eight inches tall and weighed around eleven stones. His dark brown hair was always immaculately combed back with a side parting held in place by a blob of Brylcreem. She could recall a nice friendly smiling face that she had been happy to kiss whenever she saw him. He had an unusual birthmark on his left cheek close to his eye. It resembled the letter S.

Back then his eyes had never appeared sinister or threatening. How and when did they become deep pools of evil? That thought had crossed June`s mind so many times over the passing years.

Being wrapped in cotton wool had done June no favours. Having no older siblings to set an example had left her feeling really naïve as she grew up in a world that was alien to her very prim and proper home life.

In the 1970's, the legendary Mary Whitehouse was leading her campaign to clean up television viewing and was greatly admired by June's middle class parents. Even a hint of anything sexual and the television was turned off or swiftly switched to another channel.

Herbert Sweet had worked for one of the local textile companies from first leaving school and after moving up through the ranks he had secured a managerial position in the sales department until his retirement. The job came with a decent salary and meant Gwen had never needed to work after June arrived on the scene.

Gwen had become a full time housewife and mother. She kept a very clean and extremely tidy home, which was due to her set routines for doing household chores. Furniture was polished vigorously once a week and dusted lightly almost every day. Washing was always done on Mondays and ironing the following day. Gwen took great pride in her home and often commented that visitors could call at any time of the day or night. She was never afraid to welcome anyone into her home because it was always immaculately tidy.

Appearances were always very important to Gwen. Her light brown, permed hair resembled the Queen's own hairstyle and every Friday morning at 10.00am she would take her seat at Sylvia's hair salon for a shampoo and set. Each morning, Max Factor face powder was liberally brushed over her soft features and a touch of a subtle red lipstick completed Gwen's make up regime. Her pale blue eyes were framed with very fashionable winged spectacles that gave her an air of authority. Even though she was just five feet and three inches tall and weighing a mere eight stones, anyone who met her knew she was a force to be reckoned with.

Gwen had done her utmost to make sure her neighbours and friends never had a reason to gossip about her or her family. Over the garden wall chit chat was not for her. She had blindly devoted her life to caring for her precious daughter and husband and making theirs a happy home.

Herbert was a kind and gentle man with a full head of dark brown hair, blue eyes and a lovely smile. At just a little under six feet tall and weighing a little over twelve stones he was much bigger in stature than his wife, but Gwen had always ruled the roost and he had simply allowed her to make all the decisions in June's upbringing. At times he had thought Gwen was being overly protective but knowing how much she had longed for a child Herbert knew she had only June's best interests at heart

June could not recall one swear word ever being used in the Sweet household. Gwen had her daily routines and set her own moral standards which had to be adhered to by anyone living in or visiting her home. Shoes off at the door, hands washed at mealtime and everyone must tidy up any mess they may have made were just some of the unspoken rules of the Sweet household. But as strict as Gwen could be her home was a happy one.

As June entered puberty her only advice from Gwen was vague and never to the point. Sex was a subject she had not wished to discuss, especially with her own child and the taboo subject was avoided when at all possible.

When the subject could no longer be avoided Gwen had braced herself to have a mother to daughter chat but had still not been able to explain things in simple terms. Her opening sentence had been, "Your little friend will come to visit you every month." June had pondered for days about that statement. As her only friends were at least the same height as her and Gwen rarely allowed June to have friends to stay, it made no sense to her.

When her first period finally arrived she had thankfully been prepared. Some months earlier an entire science lesson at school had been specifically about "the birds and the bees".

"Nice girls don't talk about such things," had been Gwen's response to June's innocent yet enquiring questions. Her mother had thoughtfully managed to slip a pack of sanitary towels into June's underwear drawer some months earlier but never mentioned it. Anything remotely to do with intimate parts of the body was brushed *under the carpet.*

"Keep boys at an arm's length and never bring shame upon the family," was another favourite piece of advice given to June. She had presumed it had meant not having a baby like her cousin Gloria who was only fifteen. The very mention of Gloria's name had always been accompanied by "shame" or "tut tut" and a shaking of heads.

Cousin Gloria was from Herbert's side of the family and a little older than June. There had been whispered conversations between Gwen and Herbert's sister Rose when she had visited the Sweet household a few weeks before a new addition to the family had arrived.

Rose was more in touch with the real world and though she had been bitterly disappointed and upset at Gloria's pregnancy she had been prepared to stand by her daughter. Along with her husband they had made sure mother and baby would be were well cared for.

The biological father of the baby had not been made aware of the predicament he had got Gloria into. Being only fifteen himself and the conception being caused by nothing more than a one off fumbled attempt at copulation, fuelled by natural teenage curiosity, it had been decided it was in everyone's best interest if he was not involved.

It had been one of June's classmates who had crudely explained what sex was and what the expression *"Having it off"* had actually meant. *"It"* was described by Carol Thorne as "That thing that happens between a man and a woman to make babies."

Carol Thorne was a girl who had the attention of all the young lads in her class and the reputation of being easy. It had been Carol who had taken great pleasure in giving June an insight into what *"It"* felt like.

"Hold out your left arm," Carol had said. Then, "Open up your hand." Taking hold of June's right hand she separated her middle finger from the rest and pushed it into her own mouth. Using her tongue, Carol generously covered June's finger with her saliva.

She slid the well lubricated finger from her mouth and pushed it hard against June's outstretched palm until it slid between the first and middle finger. Moving the wet finger quickly in and out between the others was Carol's demonstration of what the sex act felt like.

"See," Carol said, "there's nothing to it. "He gets a stiffy and once he's got it inside you it's over in no time. You'll need a hanky or he'll come inside you. Gets a bit messy but you don't want to have a baby do you?"

June had shuddered at the thought of doing such a ridiculous thing. The very idea made her stomach churn. A brief thought had flashed through her mind causing her to shiver as she tried to quickly put the thought out of her head. If that was what was expected of a girl when she had a boyfriend then June had decided she would be in no hurry to try "It".

On reaching sixteen, June had chosen a career in banking after gaining five GCE'O levels. Considering the stress that she had been under for years, her exam results were nothing short of a miracle. Gwen and Herbert were delighted when their beloved daughter had been offered a job at the local branch of Northern Bank. They had thought a nice and peaceful working environment would suit her to the ground.

June had passed the entrance exam for the local grammar school and been spared having to consider working in one of the many textile mills like so many of her junior school classmates who had not been as academically minded. She knew she could never have handled the jokes that she would most certainly have been the brunt of.

Having never had a boyfriend was almost like having two heads to any normal young woman. It was unheard of amongst her old classmates to not have had a boyfriend at sixteen and to still be a virgin. But a virgin was what she had wanted to be, at least mentally if not physically.

There had been one occasion and only the one, when in a bid to try and be like the other girls June had agreed to go to the cinema with a spotty faced young lad. Robbie Sedgwick had plucked up the courage to ask her out while they were sat together on the bus home from school one day.

Robbie was a bit of a social outcast at school due to having the worst case of acne anyone had seen and having had a massive spurt of growth hormones that had left him looking freakishly tall for a boy of fifteen. If nature hadn't been cruel enough to poor Robbie, having to wear spectacles and a brace on his front teeth did nothing to enhance his chances with the girls.

June had chatted with him a few times on their daily bus rides. She wasn't attracted to him but she had felt sorry for him. She had sensed he also felt a bit of an outcast. And a trip to see a film would be nothing more than a night out with a friend. How wrong could she have been?

Robbie had not been backward at coming forward when the cinema lights had dimmed. His arm had quickly slithered round the back of her seat and he had wasted no time in trying to foist his mouth full of metal onto her lips. Not wanting to draw attention to his antics, June had pulled her head away from his slobbering attempts at romance.

She quickly realised it had been a dreadful mistake by agreeing to meet him but had not expected what his next move would be. The budding Casanova had gone straight for the kill by thrusting his right hand onto her knee and swiftly moving it up her inner thigh. His immature fumbling had caused the young June to recoil in horror as she grabbed at his hand to stop him. For a split second she had been sure she was looking at a different face. A face she had tried to forget.

With emotions and familiar feelings of fear welling up inside her, June had run out of the cinema. She ran home as if her life depended on it. She never spoke to Robbie again and tried to avoid him at all costs. The feeling was probably mutual as from that night on the spurned young man never caught the same bus home again.

Like all teenage girls of that era June had photos of David Cassidy, Marc Bolan and Donny Osmond plastered over the walls of her bedroom. She could see that these idols were very good looking and loved their music, but never really understood what made young girls feel the need to scream and faint at the very sight of them. But in a need to appear normal she had followed the masses and feigned excitement at the mention of a pop idol's name. If any of her friends came to visit her at home there was never any reason for them to suspect June of being any different from them and their adolescent crushes.

In the solitude of her bedroom June would often gaze at the array of famous faces adorning the walls. Why couldn't she feel some excitement? In her darkest thoughts she already knew the answer.

Chapter 4

In her new life, it was a vibrant June who organised the girlie nights out and the Christmas parties. She would be defined by her friends as the life and soul of the party; good for a laugh.

That was the personality she had created for herself and slowly, by keeping up the pretence, it had almost become the truth, but not the whole truth.

"Morning June," was the tired response from Maureen Jones her fellow workmate as she entered the staff rest room and headed straight for the kitchen area in search of the kettle.

"My God I'm tired this morning. Hot sweats all night long and three trips to the loo. Then the bloody alarm went off just as I was nodding off. I need a cup of strong coffee. Do you want one June?"

"Why not?" June chirped, "I think we're expecting a new intake coming in today. Ginnie Barker's room is empty now and George Gilbert's is cleaned and ready for the next one. Poor old Ginnie, I liked the old girl. She still had all her marbles at home and always looked pleased to see us. Let's hope the new ones have still got some spark of life left in them." It was wishful thinking on June's part.

"God yes!" quipped Maureen. "Please don't let there be any more with incontinence problems. I seem doomed to spend my working life up to my elbows in shit and wiping arses."

"One day it could be us sat in a puddle with a toothless grin on our faces," June quickly retorted.

"You have my permission to shoot me if I ever whiff of piss and not perfume," was Maureen's immediate response as she picked up the kettle and started to fill it up from the kitchen tap.

"Jesus, talk about the power of suggestion. I run a tap and need to run to the loo. Do you reckon it's a sign of things to come?" she added with a cheeky grin.

Maureen Jones was a couple of years younger than June and had also been born and bred in the same little northern town of Burtley. Though their paths must have crossed during their earlier years neither seemed to recollect ever having met before June joined the staff at Field Hall.

June had gone to Burtley Grammar school whereas Maureen had attended the local secondary modern. From there she had gone to work in the winding department of a local textile mill like so many of her family and friends before her.

It had been through work that Maureen had met her late husband Jack. Many of her young workmates had also found their future husbands within the confines of the noisy winding sheds.

Maureen's upbringing had been so very different from the sterile environment June had been raised in. Little Mo as she had been affectionately named was the youngest of three and it had meant she had an older sister as a role model and a brother who had been very protective of his younger sibling.

By the time Maureen had reached sixteen she had already had a few boyfriends and was no stranger to quite a few sexual techniques. At nineteen she was already pregnant by her regular boyfriend, Jack Jones, and a hasty marriage had been duly arranged. Two further pregnancies followed in quick succession and her family of three sons had made her family complete.

Jack and Maureen had happily rubbed along together for over twenty years until bowel cancer had so cruelly claimed Jack's life and devastated his loving spouse. No longer able to rely on her husband for financial support Maureen had no option but to seek employment and with no special skills or academic qualifications many avenues were closed to her.

After months of nursing her beloved husband through months of palliative treatment, she had become very proficient at changing colostomy bags which had given her a good grounding for taking up a position as a care worker. No longer being squeamish at the sight of human excrement had been a real bonus when she finally secured a position at Field Hall.

Over the years June and Maureen had built up a close friendship, helping each other to adapt to their new lives as single women. The couple were physically quite different. June was tall and slim in contrast to her shorter heavier friend. It gave them a Laurel and Hardy appearance when they were together. Maureen's dark and naturally wavy hair framed her pretty face. June had been immediately drawn to her friendly smile. Her first impression of her new friend had been spot on. Maureen had a personality to match her smile and had put June at ease in her company from their first meeting. June's short, straight, fair hair gave her more defined cheekbones and jawline. She could be described as having an approachable look about her.

Maureen oozed compassion and was the type of person who you would want to turn to in times of need. Over the years June had tried so hard to adopt the best parts of her friend's personality and make them her own. Slowly, she had transformed herself from a shrinking violet into the happy go lucky person everyone now knew.

The downside of working at Field Hall was the inevitable fact that death was usually only round the corner for each and every one of the residents. Some were only there for a short period before their God called them unto him. June had spent many long nights sitting by the bedsides of the dying, holding their frail hands, determined that no one should be alone in their final hours.

June's father had battled for five years with prostate cancer, slowly deteriorating before her eyes. He had succumbed to the disease in 1990, passing away peacefully at his home. She had been present at his death and seen the comfort he'd gained from having a reassuring hand to hold onto during his final hours.

Her father had always taken a backseat to his wife when any decisions about June and her future had to be made. But, he had always shown his love for his daughter in many other ways.

Back in 1997, Gwen Sweet had died suddenly of a massive heart attack at the age of seventy five. She had been alone in her own home when her time had come not allowing her and June to say their last goodbyes.

It had been Gwen`s cleaning lady who had the misfortune of finding her body slumped in her favourite armchair. There had been some comfort for June in knowing her mother had passed away quickly and peacefully whilst watching television. Though their relationship was never full of physical hugs or kisses, June had always known she was loved and the feeling was mutual.

Day shifts at Field Hall usually passed smoothly for staff and patients with just an occasional tantrum or awkward strop from a poor soul suffering from dementia, though there were only a couple of residents in that category. Night shifts could be very unpredictable. Getting everyone to bed could be quite stressful but most of the residents would settle until the following morning. Some had been prescribed sleeping tablets to help them rest. A very vigilante eye had to be kept on the dementia sufferers, who could be prone to wandering at any hour of the day or night.

It was usually in the early hours of the morning that the frail and sick finally gasped their last breath. When June had worked night shifts, she had spent many hours holding hands with the dying.

She knew only too well the loneliness of having no one to turn in your hour of need.

Chapter 5

"Are the rooms ready for our new intake?" Mrs. McClellan, the senior manager, enquired.

"Yep, ready and waiting. What time are we expecting them to arrive here? June asked.

"As soon as the hospital can get them discharged and on their way. So, they should be here before lunchtime," her superior replied.

"Let's hope they won't be too demanding or disruptive. It would be nice to keep a little peace around here. Anything for a peaceful life," June said in a wistful voice.

It was just a few minutes past one o'clock when the first new resident arrived in an ambulance. Ellen Gregson was eighty two years old and had suffered a few nasty falls in the past year. Her frail body had taken a battering with her last fall and it had been decided she was no longer able to live alone. So, she had agreed to go into residential care. Her home had been a rented council bungalow and her closest relative being her niece, had packed up Ellen's most personal belongings for her and terminated her tenancy.

The remainder of her furniture had been given away to some charity shop.

June instinctively knew that Ellen would be no trouble. She had come to recognise who could be problematic and which residents would settle in easily. Ellen's room was decorated exactly the same as every other in the home in a pastel green emulsion on the walls and white paintwork. Curtains with various shades of green swirls in the pattern completed the decor. All the resident's rooms were pleasing on the eye and could be made to look quite cosy when a few personal possessions were added to the basic light wood furniture. A few treasured photographs along with a few favourite ornaments usually helped the residents to feel at home very quickly.

It was about an hour later when the second of the new residents arrived by ambulance. This was an old man who had suffered a severe stroke and had not regained the use of his right arm. His speech had been reduced to nothing more than grunts and groans. He had managed to regain sufficient strength in his legs to manage shuffling a few feet with some assistance.

There was nothing more to be gained by keeping him in hospital once his condition had stabilised. Having no close relatives to care for him he had no option than to be taken into a home where he could be properly looked after.

The elderly man was being wheeled from the ambulance by a paramedic who had strapped him into a transfer chair for the short journey from the vehicle to the reception area. Sarah Stead was one of Field Hall's state registered nurses and was walking alongside the new resident, clutching his discharge papers, medical records and a small suitcase.

June was in the reception area as the old man was being wheeled in. She turned around to greet him with a friendly smile as she always tried to do whenever they had a new arrival.

Her facial muscles froze and time seemed to stand still as she glanced at the face of the old man being ushered past her. Her whole body had become suddenly weak and her heart started to race.

"June. Are you feeling okay? You've turned quite pale. You look as if you've just seen a ghost," Sarah Stead said as she walked past her.

"No. I feel a bit dizzy Sarah. It'll be my blessed hormones playing up again. I'll go sit down for a minute or two. It'll pass. I might have a cup of sweet tea. That might help," June had hesitantly replied.

As she closed the door to the staff kitchen behind her, June felt herself starting to shake. She was thankful there were no other staff members around to see her hands tremble as she struggled to fill the kettle for a much needed sugary drink. Something a bit stronger like a brandy would have been very welcome to calm her nerves, but sweet tea had to suffice. Sweet tea would raise her blood sugar levels and hopefully help her to fool everyone in to thinking that her hormonal problem really was the reason for her strange behaviour. No one could ever know the real cause of her funny turn.

Chapter 6

The clock on the mantelpiece chimes five o` clock. He feels his heart starting to beat faster. The palms of his hands have started to perspire. He is so familiar with the signs of sexual tension and eager anticipation.

He peers from behind the yellowing net curtains that veil his leaded living room window, eyes searching anxiously for the familiar figure to come into view. She`s was always on time and right on cue she opens the garden gate and walks slowly towards the front door. The door opens before she has a chance to ring the bell. The young girl steps inside like a lamb to the slaughter.

"Come in dear, let me take your coat," he says with a wide smile on his face.

"Thank you," she faintly mumbles.

As they walk towards the piano standing in the far corner of the room, she notices a cine projector mounted on a tripod. Fastened to the wall of an alcove there`s a large white screen used for showing home movies. She`s never seen the camera before, even though she has been in the room many times.

Wearing her school uniform of a green and white gingham dress, green cardigan and white ankle socks she looks so innocent. A matching green ribbon in her long dark brown hair makes her look so angelic and pure. He notes that she has her hair in a single plait, not her usual two. It doesn`t matter to him as long as her young flawless face isn`t covered.

"Let`s get started shall we dear," he says as he put his arms upon her small shoulders and ushers her towards the old upright piano. "Have you been practising like a good girl? Now let`s start with the scales and get those nimble fingers nicely stretched."

She sits on the piano stool and lifts the lid to expose the old and yellowing keyboard.

He has the familiar stirrings in his groin. Standing closely behind her he admires her slender frame with the long plait flowing down her back. Unable to resist touching her bare neck with his clammy fingers he towers over her. He has fantasised about this moment for weeks. The urges he has held inside him have become so intense. He is no longer in control of his actions.

The girl's fingers are shaking slightly as she tries to press down the piano keys. He sees this as his cue to move closer to her young body.

"Stand up my dear. I can help you to get the fingering just right if I sit on the stool and you sit here before me," he says with laboured breath. "Come, you sit here and I will guide your hands."

He wraps his hands around her tiny waist and eases her backwards onto the stool so she is sitting between his legs. As her body comes into contact with his he feels the tingling of his erection intensifying as his penis swells a little more. Every small movement she makes sends shivers through his body. He can't stop himself from wrapping his arms around her and pushing his groin even closer to her body.

His breathing is heavier and faster as he holds her wrists above the keyboard. The fresh soapy aroma of her hair fills his nostrils. She wriggles her body, trying to move forward and out of the grip of his thighs. Each move she makes caused him to shudder and take him closer to the inevitable orgasm he so badly yearns for.

With shaking hands she tries to remember which keys to play, knowing that if she plays one wrong note she will give him a reason to move his body even closer to her. His arms are wrapped around her and she is now unable to break free.

Feeling his hot breath on her neck makes her more uncomfortable. The sounds he makes remind her of a dog panting but she does not understand why.

With every second that passes she concentrates only on placing her small fingers on the right keys, just wanting the lesson to end. As she plays the final notes from the music manuscript his arms tighten around her waist. He shudders and makes strange groaning noises before he releases his grip on her waist and quietly whispers, "Well done".

At last she is able to move away from the piano and make her way towards the front door.

"Same time next week my dear. Don't forget to practise every single day," he says as he holds out her coat. Opening the front door he leans towards her face and kisses her gently on her cheek.

She avoids looking him in the face as she puts on her coat and steps outside. With her head bowed and staring at the pavement, through teary eyes, the young girl starts her short walk home.

Chapter 7

Monday March 4th 2012

Had she just seen a ghost? Or was it just a trick of the light that was shining very brightly through the reception area windows? She would have to go back and take another look at their new male resident and see if she really had seen that distinctive brown birthmark. There couldn`t possibly be two men with such a distinguishing mark down the side of his left cheek that was shaped like the letter S. Or could there?

Trying to think rationally, June decided she needed to find out his name and background information. "I will have to get a look at his medical records," she said out loud, then "What excuse can I use if I get caught with them?" Her thoughts were interrupted by her friend Maureen opening the kitchen door.

"How are you feeling? Sarah said you had a funny turn earlier. Not got a lot going for it this menopause lark. Has it?"

"I`m still a bit shaky but it will pass. It was a pretty bad welcome I gave the old man this morning. I never got to speak to him or ask his name," June answered hoping she sounded convincing whilst willing Maureen to give her the vital name she needed to know.

"I doubt he even noticed you. He`s probably just glad to be out of the hospital. No relatives as such. He never got married. Think someone said he`s called Denis Goodman or something like that," Maureen said, unknowingly confirming June`s sickening suspicions.

She was still feeling the effects of her earlier adrenalin rush when her heart began racing again. It felt as if her head would explode as the room seemed to sway and her legs became unsteady.

So she had seen a ghost. A ghost from her past that she had thought had been exorcised years ago.

After a strong cup of sweet tea and a quiet half hour alone in the staff rest room, June`s pulse rate finally slowed down to somewhere near normal. Though still feeling lightheaded she was able to collect her thoughts.

The unusual birthmark, she knew could have been a coincidence but not the name as well. It just had to be him. She had imagined he would be dead by now. In fact she had hoped he had met a rather sticky end as was befitting of him. It appeared not.

She knew that their meeting again was inevitable and needed to get her act together before it happened. He must never sense her apprehension when they met, nor should any member of staff. It would take an Oscar winning acting performance on June's part to carry it off. Could she do it?

"Course you can," June mumbled to herself. "You've been acting most of your life girl."

With that thought, an air of calmness replaced her fears and the beginnings of a sly grin became visible on her pasty face. She took a couple of slow deep breaths and rose from the armchair she had flopped into a little while earlier.

"On with the show. Act one, scene one," she said in a rather determined tone of voice.

"Right, panic over. Normal service is resumed," June announced as she walked back into the reception area. "Have we finished serving lunch? I'll make a start on clearing up then."

With shoulders pulled back and holding her head high June walked from the reception area into the dining room. Using every ounce of willpower she could muster, she stopped her eyes from searching out Denis Goodman. Nonchalantly, she walked up to a few of the residents and started making mundane chit chat.

Moving slowly from one familiar face to another, collecting their dirty plates and cutlery, she manoeuvred around the dining room in a casual manner. Then, without turning her head she knew instantly that he was sitting only a few feet away.

If there was such a thing as sixth sense, then that was exactly what she was experiencing. A sudden cold shiver ran down her spine.

Just managing to keep her composure she turned to face an elderly man with obvious signs of partial paralysis of his face. The familiar lop sided jaw and tell-tale dribbles of saliva from the right side of his mouth were not enough to make his face unrecognisable. A few broken liquorice coloured teeth were just visible.

There was no mistaking the unusual birthmark close to his left eye. Deep brown eyes that had once been so hypnotic and able to make June feel helpless and afraid had lost most of their colour. His once dark brown hair was now almost white with just a peppering of grey. The chiselled features she remembered so clearly were now more skeletal and sallow.

There was very little left of the once mesmerising and penetrating windows to his soul, but enough to make June feel uncomfortable as she forced herself to smile at him.

"Hello, I'm June. You must be Denis our new resident," she said through a broad smile and gritted teeth. "We're a happy bunch here. You'll soon settle in and make friends. There's a lot of food left on your plate Denis. Would you like me to help you eat a little more?"

Taking a fork in her hand June scooped up a small amount of mashed potato and offered it to Denis. He opened his mouth ready for her to feed it to him fully exposing his few broken and discoloured molars. After a couple more mouthfuls he raised his frail and shaking left hand making it clear he had eaten enough of his lunch.

Now I have got him eating out of my hand, was the first thought that came into June's head. *He'll eat more than humble pie when I've finished with him,* was her second.

As she scooped up the plate of cold food June looked Denis straight in the eye and said, "We're going to get on well Denis. I'll be seeing you later."

With those words and a wry smile she turned away and headed towards the trolley full of dirty plates.

It was around 6.15pm when June arrived home. As she closed the door to her small apartment she let out a deep sigh. Dropping her shopping bag in the hall and not bothering to take off her coat and shoes she headed straight into her living room.

23

With an unsteady hand she pulled open the door of her teak sideboard and reached inside to grab a bottle that she had been storing for years. She reached for a glass tumbler with her other hand and placed it on the top of the sideboard.

"Time for some serious thinking June," she said out loud to herself as she unscrewed the top off the bottle of brandy and proceeded to pour herself a large measure.

As the first mouthful slid down her throat she gave out another large sigh. With the second gulp a soothing warm sensation eased the tightening in her chest that had been gripping her since first setting eyes on Denis Goodman.

A few more gulps of the brandy that she had always kept for purely medicinal purposes and the glass was empty. She reached out again for the bottle with her shaky hand and poured another glassful. Her coat and shoes were strewn upon the soft, beige carpeted living room floor.

Flopping down onto her much cherished chocolate brown sofa, her hand retained a firm grip of the glass. June tossed her head backwards feeling the coolness of the leather against her cheek. She loved the sofa she had saved so hard for. Curling up on the comfy cushions to watch her favourite soap operas was her way of unwinding at the end of a working day. Today she had needed that comfort and a stiff drink more than ever. What had started out as just another day had suddenly developed into a living nightmare.

Nightmares were usually short lived and quickly forgotten but June knew she was not going to wake up and find that this had been just a bad dream. She was going to have to face her bogey man every working day. That very thought prompted her stomach to churn and her pulse to start racing again.

June downed the contents of the glass in one large gulp then closed her eyes hoping it would allow her to clear her muddled brain. She was starting to feel light headed and suddenly very sleepy.

Within seconds June had let the empty glass slip from her hand as she drifted into deep slumber.

Chapter 8

The familiar chiming of the clock on the mantelpiece has set his pulse racing. It's five o'clock and he waits for the familiar knocking on his front door. Each passing second seems like an hour.

The past week has seemed like a month. Each night he has fantasised about feeling her soft young flesh close to his again. The smell of her hair has lingered in his nostrils like a French perfume. He yearns to hold her; caress her.

At five minutes past the hour the girl slowly walks up the path. Her clenched fist hovers a few seconds before making the first knock at the door. At the sound of the latch turning she feels the muscles of her stomach beginning to tighten.

The girl plays the set pieces from the manuscripts, propped up on the old piano, she's constantly aware of him hovering behind her.

For the past week she has fervently practised each small exercise he has given her to do, hoping that if she is able to play them well she will not give him any excuse to sit beside her on the piano stool.

After almost an hour of playing scales and short melodies he's made no attempt to sit close to her, which has been a relief to the young girl. Then he calmly says, "That will be enough for today. I'm very pleased with your progress and think maybe we should be putting you forward for your first exam. Pack up your music and we will discuss it." He places his hands upon her shoulders and slides them gently down to her chest.

She closes her eyes as a shudder runs down her spine. His hands have started moving in a slow circular motion over the fabric of her school dress covering her slightly developed breasts.

The feel of her budding nipples through the cotton fabric has set off a stirring in his groin. His fantasy is now almost a reality.

Moving his sweating palms back up to her shoulders, he gently wraps them around her bare arms and ushers her away from the piano stool, steering her towards his grubby old sofa in the middle of the room. A dusty two barred electric fire, housed in an old tiled fireplace, is providing just enough heat to keep the musty room from feeling cold and dank.

"Sit down my dear. Now, I think it's time to consider taking your first exam," he says in a gentle whisper as he sits down close beside her. "Do you think you're ready to take the test dear? We can have extra time together to make sure you are fully prepared if you wish. Would you like that?"

Before the girl can answer, he's placed his left hand upon her knees and started to pat them gently whilst his other arm slides across her shoulders. She is being pulled even closer towards him.

"You know how fond of you I am dear and how proud your parents will be if you gain a certificate," he says quietly, as his piercing dark brown eyes meet hers. Sliding his hand from her bare knee, he moves it slowly up to her thigh.

The bulge in his trousers has become obvious to her. She stiffens at the touch of his cold, clammy fingers snaking under the elasticated seam of her thick green cotton knickers. He's taking no notice of the girl's attempts to pull back his hand and thrust his fingers even further, until he feels the soft moist flesh of her most private parts.

Ignoring the girl's protests, he holds her face close to his chest and continues exploring the contours of her genitals. Oblivious to any discomfort that his probing fingers are causing her, he continues to push harder and deeper. No longer able to hold back an orgasmic release his climax comes to fruition. He lets out a deep sigh and pulls his hand away from her thigh.

Staring deep into her young, blue eyes, welling up with tears, he quietly mutters, "This will be just our special little secret dear. You know what keeping a secret means don't you? I will help you through your exams if you are nice to your uncle Denis. Now run along home and tell your parents how well you have done today. Remember, it's just our little secret."

He places a kiss on the top of her head and inhales the sweet smell of her hair again before he opens the door.

"Until next week my dear," are words she has come to dread.

On the short walk back to her home the girl stares continually at the pavement, unable to bring herself to look up. Will her parents be able to tell that she is keeping a secret?

Will they be able to see in her eyes what she has just done? How can she avoid being alone with him ever again?

Chapter 9

June's alcohol induced sleep was suddenly disturbed by the piercing ring tone of her mobile phone. Bleary eyed and slightly confused she tried to clear her head and find out where the annoying shrill of Dolly Parton belting out "Nine to Five" was coming from. Stumbling and fumbling about on her plush beige carpet she finally found the source of the annoying song at the bottom of her handbag. Hastily pressing the green button made the music cease.

"Hello!" she mumbled, still half asleep.

"June, it's me Maureen. I was just checking you were okay. You looked ever so pale this afternoon. I wondered if you were sickening for something. I know you blamed your blessed hormones but you looked really odd, spaced out even."

"Yeah, I'm fine now. Hormones or not it's passed now. I'll try and get an early night. That should help. But thanks for worrying about me. I'll see you tomorrow," June replied as calmly as she could.

"Okay, see you then. Goodnight June," her friend said with her voice still full of concern for her close pal.

Being fully roused from her sleep June made her way into her compact kitchen and headed straight towards the kettle. A cup of coffee to clear her head was the foremost thought in her mind.

Whilst going through the familiar motions of making her much needed caffeine fix, her thoughts returned to the face that she had tried to forget for almost forty years. Even though his features were now distorted with partial paralysis and his eyes had lost their deep brown penetrating glare, just the thought of having to look at him again was starting to make bile rise up into the back of her throat.

Cupping the mug of hot coffee in her hands, June realised how cold she was feeling. The warmth being generated from her favourite china mug was soothing to her palms and fingers. Reaching out to check that the central heating was on she placed her hand on the kitchen radiator. June knew the cold that was engulfing her body was coming from within. Not only was her body feeling numb but the thoughts racing through her mind were coming so fast that she could not think straight, making her brain unable to function clearly. She knew she had to take control over her actions and not let Denis Goodman's evil presence overpower her ever again.

After her divorce from Nigel and realising she needed to rise from her depressed state of mind, June had sought help in the form of hypnosis. A few sessions of hypnotherapy had proved invaluable before she had started work at Field Hall. She would never be able to forget her deep rooted problems but with the wonderful coaxing and support of her hypnotherapist, June had been able to put the horrible memories behind her and move forward in life. It wasn't a case of just healing her wounds but learning to deal with them.

Her therapy sessions had often been almost as upsetting as the actual abuse when she was helped to regress and describe the emotions she had felt at the hands of her uncle, Denis Goodman.

At each weekly session June had succumbed to the reassuring voice of her therapist and was guided into a fully relaxed state of mind and body .Gently she had been asked to remember specific and explicit details of her abuse and abuser. Reliving the experiences had been the only way to help June change her subconscious mind into believing she had not been to blame for any of her abuser's disgusting actions. She was the innocent victim and had no cause to feel ashamed. That was the message that had been slowly and patiently implanted into her disturbed conscience.

Eventually the manipulative skills of her therapist had helped June to overcome her feelings of shame and fill her mind with new emotions. She had felt her depression lifting and more positive thoughts replacing the old tormenting ones that had been with her for so long. She had actually started to think about her future with enthusiasm and with her new found confidence had started her new life as a single person.

Now, June felt as if all the progress she had made in her new life was about to be destroyed and Denis would once again overpower her with his very presence. She could not let it happen to her all over again and a strong feeling of determination was beginning to take place in her muddled brain.

That evening the television had been nothing more than a familiar background noise. Her favourite soap characters had played out their dramas to one totally disinterested viewer.

Thoughts had passed through June`s head like an express train going through a tunnel as she tried so hard not to recall the memories which she thought had been buried forever. But no amount of willpower could stop them.

Exhausted by the turmoil of the day June turned off the television, checked the door to her flat was locked and the security chain was firmly in position. Turning off all the lights as she moved through each room June finally closed the bedroom door behind her.

Doubting that she would have a restful night`s sleep, June`s eyes came to rest on the bedside cabinet. Knowing what was inside the cabinet, she was unable to resist the lure of a small bottle of sleeping tablets. The bottle of pills had been left at the back of the cabinet untouched for years. It had been the prescription pills that had helped June get through her divorce. Just one little pill at night had guaranteed her a few hours respite from the worry and strain of her break up with Nigel.

The use by date was well in the past but she could not see what harm they could do. That was the most prominent thought in June`s head as she opened the cabinet door and reached into the back of the bottom shelf. With the little brown bottle clutched firmly in her fist she shook out one of her "little helpers". June swallowed the little white tablet with the help of a large mouthful of water from the plastic bottle that stood on the top of the cabinet. Sleep would hopefully come soon.

Chapter 10

He holds her wrists gently and leads her towards the old worn sofa again. Dread creeps up on her with each small step she takes.

"Let's sit down shall we dear? I do look forward to our lessons. You're such a good girl for your favourite uncle."

Her small body is squashed against the arm of the sofa as her legs tremble with the anticipation of what is about to happen. A burning sensation in the back of her throat brings on the familiar taste of bile and a feeling of nausea.

She looks down and casts a glance from the corners of her eyes at his unbuttoned trousers and fears what is to come. His right arm snakes behind her and across her shoulders coming to rest at the nape of her neck. His left hand slips into the gaping hole in his trousers and frees his swollen penis.

She closes her eyes in a desperate attempt to make the sight of the disgusting thing disappear. Tears well in her eyes as a tightening sensation grips her chest.

Gently stroking her right cheek he whispers, "You want to make me happy dear don't you? You know how to make me happy, so very happy."

His hand moves from her cheek and takes a firm grip of the back of her head. The pressure of his hand forces her head down and towards his lap. Keeping her eyes tightly shut she can offer little resistance and knows it is useless to struggle. Any strength she had has been drained by fear.

The disgusting piece of flesh fills her mouth and her gagging reflex kicks in. Feeling sick and light headed she is barely aware of anything other than a desperate need to clear her throat. Suddenly, her mouth is filled with a hot slimy substance that she does not want to try and swallow.

He releases the grip on her head and pulls the limp piece of flesh from her mouth. She tries spitting out the slime from her mouth as he hands her a grubby handkerchief.

"Wipe your face my dear. You are such a good girl and you must remember this is our very special little secret dear," he says in a quiet yet haunting tone of voice.

She can`t bring herself to look at him. The familiar piercing stare from his deep brown eyes are imbedded in her mind and she knows they always will be.

Her short walk home takes longer than usual as the girl stops twice with the urge to vomit. But her retching only amounts to a bout of spitting sour saliva. The need to wash out her mouth and clear the disgusting residue becomes overwhelming.

Finally reaching her home, she closes the front door and runs straight upstairs to the privacy of the bathroom. In the safety of the small room she puts her mouth to the cold water tap and turns the head to start a trickle she so badly needs to wash away any remaining semen. No amount of swilling will take away the taste or the urge to be sick.

After a while her odd behaviour in the bathroom comes to the notice of her mother who shows immediate concern and starts to ask awkward questions. She is unable to answer her truthfully.

Convinced her daughter is simply suffering from a mild throat infection, she offers her a glass of warm salty water to gargle and help sooth her throat. Unable to contradict her mother`s misguided assumption, the girl dutifully washes her mouth out with the saline solution and starts to retch again.

Declining any food and allowing her parents to believe she is feeling ill, she seeks solace in her bedroom. Huddled beneath the sheets of her single bed she allows her tears to flood like a waterfall flowing over the contours of her face.

Clenching her fists so hard, her fingernails cut into the soft skin of her palms. Yet she feels no pain.

Chapter 11

Tuesday 5th March 2012

Bleary eyed and only half conscious June struggled to make out the time displayed on her digital alarm clock which was only a few inches away from her face. The illuminated red numbers glowed brightly in the darkness of her bedroom and read 4.37am. The sleeping pill had done its job for a short time at least, but her induced slumber had not been peaceful. For the first time in years Denis Goodman had crept into her dreams and her dream that night had become a nightmare.

Fully awake she could sense the over powering feelings of disgust and shame returning. She had battled for almost forty years to put all thoughts of Denis Goodman out of her mind and now here he was again, still able to make her feel guilty and full of self-loathing.

But this time things would be different. June had decided that the evil, perverted creature hiding inside the shell of a frail old man was not going to have the upper hand. She was not about to let him ruin the life she now had. He had robbed her of being able to form a decent relationship with men and been the cause of her marriage breaking up.

Because of his actions June had been deprived of ever having a normal family life with a husband and children. She would have loved to have had children. He had caused her to detach herself from everyone she had ever loved.

Never being able to tell her parents of the abuse Denis Goodman had deemed it his right to inflict upon her had often caused more emotional turmoil than just the shame she had felt.

To Gwen and Herbert Sweet, their daughter had grown up into an awkward young lady. For weeks after she had insisted she stopped having her piano lessons, June never wanted to be around at family gatherings, preferring to stay in her room.

Regular visits to her grandparent's home had always been something June had looked forward to. They lived approximately twenty miles away in a small town called Milsden. Gwen's parents, Gladys and Albert Goodman had been typical doting grandparents and had always been so proud of their only granddaughter.

On every visit, Gladys would prepare a special tea of ham salad with tinned fruit and cream in the summer months or in winter she dished up one of her homemade stews followed by bread and butter pudding smothered with custard. These special meals were always looked forward to by their young granddaughter.

June had loved her grandparents dearly. Gladys was a homely woman who always wore a pinafore and covered her grey hair with a hairnet. On special occasions she would have her hair done at the local hairdresser's and apply a little make up to her soft rounded face. A splash of Lily of the Valley scent completed her beauty routine.

The one consistent thing June could always remember about her grandma was a faint smell of peppermint on her breath when she kissed her. Even decades later the smell of peppermint always brought back memories of Gladys and the happy times June had spent with her.

Albert Sweet had been a quiet man who wasn't a great conversationalist and spent most of his time saying, "yes dear" to Gladys. He was average height but had a wiry physique in contrast to his pleasantly plump wife.

In the summer months he always appeared to have a sun tan which faded in the winter months to leave his skin with a sallow yellowy appearance. He had retained a full head of hair all his life and it was only very late in life that his dark brown hair turned grey.

June's fondest memories of her granddad were the smell of Brylcreem on his hair and the aroma of his pipe tobacco which he was rarely seen without.

The joys of visiting her only two grandparents were permanently marred from the day Denis Goodman sexually abused his niece for the first time. Whenever the Sweet family made a visit to Milsden, Denis was always asked to go along with them. He did not drive and

Gwen felt it only natural that her brother should be at the regular family gatherings.

June had sacrificed as many visits as she could to avoid being sat in their car with him. She hated him for the lies she had to tell and the disappointment of not seeing the old couple she loved so much.

Herbert Sweet's parents had died before June was born. His father had died because of a war injury and his mother had died of cancer when Herbert was in his late teens. June had very few relatives and Denis Goodman's behaviour had stopped her seeing most of them.

Gladys and Albert would have been devastated if they had known their only son was a paedophile. If they had known that his chosen victim was their precious granddaughter, the upset may well have sent them to early graves. Their lives would have been shattered, as would their daughter Gwen's if she had ever known.

There had only been one casualty to come out of the whole sordid business and that was June.

Insisting on giving up piano lessons for no apparent reason after her parents had saved so hard to buy a piano made her seem an ungrateful child. Simply having to tell them so many lies to explain away her behaviour over the passing years had made her relationship with her loving parents very strained at times.

June had often come close to blurting out the truth about the reasons behind her odd reactions. She had spent many hours in her bedroom working out just what to say to her parents about the piano lessons. But would they have believed her? Having to explain the sickening behaviour of her uncle would have been as upsetting as actually being abused all over again. But the fact that it was her uncle responsible for the disgusting attacks would most certainly have devastated her parents.

From being a toddler June's uncle had been a regular visitor to her home and she had many happy memories of her time spent with him which had been later replaced by hatred. He had even been chosen to be her Godfather when she was christened. He had made vows to God, in a church, to look after his niece.

It was much later in her life that June remembered his odd behaviour towards her as a child. After having hypnotherapy she had experienced memory flashbacks.

June had long hair and usually had her shiny brown locks plaited during her school years. It had never struck her as odd that her uncle loved to brush her hair whenever he visited their home and to do it he would pull her up close and clamp her body between his legs.

Even her mother Gwen had appeared to be oblivious to any of his unusual actions when he was around her daughter. Herbert Sweet had never taken it upon himself to plait his daughter's hair, but Denis loved to do it.

It was only when she was approaching puberty that June noticed Denis had started to behave differently towards her. He had always given her cuddles and kisses but later on started to grab her and pull her towards him, which always resulted in her sitting on his lap. June had started feeling ill at ease with his more intimate actions but at that point he hadn't started to touch her or do anything in a specifically sexual manner. Even her first few piano lessons had gone accordingly and Denis had concentrated only on passing on his musical skills. That was all to change forever.

The Christmas of 1971 had been totally ruined for June and became an exceptionally awkward one for her parents. Being totally oblivious of the torment that her brother Denis had been inflicting on her daughter during the past weeks, Gwen had invited her younger sibling to spend Christmas day with the Sweet family.

That was nothing unusual as Denis had always spent Christmas with them. But on being told the news that her Uncle Denis was to be their house guest yet again over that particular festive period had freaked June out.

In the run up to Christmas, Gwen had spent her time planning the dinner menu and shopping for gifts. As her mother's excitement mounted poor June had slipped into a deeper depression and state of panic. How was she to avoid her abuser without making it so obvious to her parents? That had been June's most prominent thought.

A couple of days before the big day, June had finally decided her best option was to fake an illness that would give her the excuse not to have to spend any time in Denis's company. To avert any suspicion about her intentions June started to construct her little plot.

Firstly, with a couple of days to go before the festivities were to start, June casually mentioned to Gwen that she had a headache and was feeling very weak. A couple of Anadin tablets had been dispensed and duly swallowed without causing much concern.

Keeping up the deceit the following day had taken the form of June speaking in a low and frail voice and constantly mentioning how much her throat and neck were hurting. Again, the symptoms were believable enough but not too concerning for her mother.

Christmas Eve arrived and that had called for a bit more acting on June's part. She had been forced into puffing out her cheeks and making her face look as if it was slightly swollen. Coupled with the symptoms of a sore throat and painful neck she hoped it may appear she had developed swollen glands or even Mumps. She had heard the latter could be quite serious to adult males.

Gwen had mentioned calling in their doctor but June had insisted she would be fine as long as she could stay in bed and rest. Eventually it had been agreed that she should remain in her room until she felt better. Gwen had been bitterly disappointed at the thought of her daughter having to miss the Christmas dinner she had planned.

June had shivered at the sound of the doorbell ringing in the late afternoon of Christmas Eve. Hearing muffled voices downstairs meant that their guest had arrived. Would he suspect she was deliberately trying to avoid him?

Praying that Denis would not want to come up and see his niece in her bedroom, June hoped he would not want to risk a dose of Mumps either. When Gwen took up a tray with some food on and was obviously alone, June was able to breathe a sigh of relief.

That Christmas Eve was a quiet affair at the Sweet's home and having the luxury of a small portable television in June's bedroom had meant she was able to view whatever she chose to in privacy and relative safety. She had the forethought to stash a few tasty snacks in her wardrobe so she didn't miss out on a festive feast in her quest to convince everyone she was really ill.

When the family retired to bed that night June was uncomfortably aware that her abuser was sleeping in the bedroom next to hers. As she huddled in the comfort of her bed she could clearly hear sounds coming from the adjoining room. A sickening thought had flashed through her brain. Would he try to creep into her room when he thought everyone would be sleeping soundly?

In an instant June had jumped out of bed and scanned the room for something to push against the bedroom door. An armchair in the corner of her room had been easy enough to slide across the carpet and wedge against the door handle.

Knowing that Denis would not be able to even try and sneak into her room without waking everyone had made June relax sufficiently to try and get some sleep. Christmas day was to bring more challenges in her quest to avoid their houseguest.

The following morning June was awakened by familiar noises coming from the bathroom. The sound of their toilet flushing had her leaping out of bed to slide the armchair back into the corner of her room. Knowing that it wouldn't be long before Gwen came to her room to check on her she huddled back into her bed. Though feeling perfectly well she had to keep up the pretence of still being ill for at least one more day.

As expected, Gwen entered the small bedroom without knocking to check up on her sick daughter and wish her a Merry Christmas. After another convincing performance on June's part her mother had accepted that bed would be the best place for her to stay for another day. Feelings of guilt and relief ran parallel through June's mind. She was spoiling her mother's efforts to have a family Christmas but no way could she have ever sat at the dining table in such close proximity to a man she despised so much.

The day passed slowly for her. Whenever she heard the sound of footsteps coming up the stairs her heart skipped a beat. Would he decide to stick his head round the door to speak to her? Would he be brazen enough to enter her room unannounced? These and many more frightening thoughts constantly raced through her brain the whole day.

38

Gwen had brought June a pile of presents for her to open all lovingly wrapped in colourful paper. A tray with a plate full of their festive dinner on had followed, being carefully carried by her father Herbert wearing a flimsy red paper hat in the shape of a crown. Herbert offered June a Christmas cracker to pull which she did and made a wish. Both parents had wished her a "Merry Christmas" and expressed their disappointment at not having their daughter to dine with them and their guest.

Uncle Denis had sent his love and "Compliments of the season" but it had been thought best he did not risk getting infected with Mumps and so he had chosen not to enter June`s bedroom. Her bedroom had become the only place June could feel safe, and she did not want her vile uncle intruding on her only bit of privacy.

It was late evening when June was finally able to breathe a sigh of relief when her mother called out to tell her that Denis was leaving and that he hoped she was much better very soon. At least she would be able to stop the pretence and spend Boxing Day in the usual way.

On the dressing table in her bedroom was a gift box which she had opened, but on reading the attached card to it she had discarded it immediately. Denis had written, *For my very special niece, from your loving uncle. xx* The gift was a silver charm bracelet with two charms attached. It was one piece of jewellery that she vowed she would not wear and didn`t except for just one occasion.

Making sure that her mother had caught sight of the silver bracelet, June wore it for the first and only time to go shopping for clothes in the January sales. As she tried on various items of clothing she used the privacy of a changing cubicle to remove the bracelet and slip it into her pocket. Gwen waited patiently for her daughter to emerge from behind the curtain oblivious to her cunning capers.

Later that day June broke the news to her mother that her bracelet was missing. The conclusion was made that it must have been lost whilst trying on clothes and it could be anywhere. Gwen insisted that June should not tell her uncle about the loss as it may upset him. She gladly agreed to keep the secret knowing that the gift she despised so much had been deliberately and discreetly dropped into a waste bin on the journey home from the shops.

Chapter 12

Would they have believed that Gwen's younger brother was capable of such depravity? Would he have denied it all and accused June of being an attention seeking liar?

These questions had gone round and round in June's mind. These had become questions that would never be answered.

June received the best possible news in late January of 1972. Denis Goodman had announced to his family he was to move out of the area. It was only a few months after June stopped having her piano lessons. His excuse for moving had been a simple one. He had cheerfully told his sister and her husband that he'd been given a chance to teach piano in a school in the outskirts of London. It was supposedly too good an opportunity for him to miss.

Gwen had been upset at the news but delighted for her little brother who she had always felt extremely close to. So, she asked no questions and simply believed the yarn he had spun her. Within a couple of weeks, 26, Lower Burtley Road, Denis's rented terrace house had been emptied of all furniture and June's abuser had moved on to pastures new.

Promises to keep in touch were made by both siblings but after a few short phone calls made in the first weeks of his move Denis had never kept his promise. When his phone calls ceased and Gwen's calls never answered, she wrote numerous letters to the address she'd been given. There had never been any acknowledgement of her many letters except on one occasion when a letter was returned "Not at this address". And so to her dying day she had no idea where he was living.

June had always suspected the job had been a pack of lies and that he was running away before he was exposed of his despicable behaviour and had hoped with all her heart that he would never make contact with his sister again. When he had made no contact for over two years she tried to convince herself he was gone for ever and it was safe to get on with her life. She had often wondered if any other of his other pupils had been subjected to his sickening advances or had she been the only one?

If she had felt unable to overcome the shame and tell her parents, then there probably were others feeling exactly the same. Dirty, soiled and guilty of allowing him to touch her were only a few of the emotions June had felt wash over her numerous times a day. Though he had gone from her life she had never plucked up the courage to reveal her secret and continued to carry the burden alone.

When Nigel Cowburn entered June's life she had been at a low ebb. He had been promoted to the position of Assistant Manager at Burtley's branch of Northern Bank. His promotion had meant him moving from the Midlands to the small industrial town.

Being a stranger to the community he had turned to June for advice and information about his new home surroundings and being born and bred in Burtley she had been happy to help.

His gentle nature had won her over and she'd thought she had finally found a member of the opposite sex who did not make her feel so ill at ease. Slowly their relationship had grown from being simply work mates into a warm and comfortable courtship.

June had hoped that if their relationship was allowed to grow at a slow pace she would, in time, be able to accept Nigel's physical expressions of affection for her and even demonstrate her feelings for him.

After four years of being a couple, June had been unable to fob Nigel off with any more excuses not to get married. And so a small wedding at the local registry office had been arranged for August 12th 1995.

After the short ceremony a few family members and friends returned to June's parent's home for a typical finger buffet. Oblivious to the effect it would have on her daughter, Gwen had commented on how sad it was that June's father and uncle were not with them to celebrate. Sadly, Herbert had passed away before seeing his daughter married. All the guests had agreed but before any further comments could be made the bride quickly changed the subject.

"I think it's time we cut the wedding cake," had steered everyone's attentions away from Denis's absence.

Their wedding had gone smoothly and though it had been a very quiet affair both her and Nigel had enjoyed their special day.

June had chosen to wear a light grey polyester two piece suit with a pastel yellow satin blouse which flattered her slim figure. A pair of high heeled, grey court shoes had complimented her shapely legs.

June's hairdresser had used her imagination and blow dried her client's usually straight hair into a very flattering style. Carrying a small posy of yellow roses June had been transformed from the frumpy looking bank clerk into an attractive blushing bride.

Their wedding night was spent at their new home. A two bedroomed terraced house, rented from a local landlord, had been sparsely furnished but the couple had still managed to make it feel like a cosy little home.

A brand new double bed covered with a pretty set of bed linen and a soft duvet almost filled the tiny bedroom. This was where the long wait to consummate their relationship was to come to an end and had been one of great expectations for the eager groom but full of anxious anticipation for the shy young bride. In the comfort of their new bed, June and Nigel took their first steps towards what was expected to be a long and loving marriage.

Nigel had been a very patient boyfriend and June knew that he genuinely loved her. Like any normal red blooded male he had naturally wanted a physical relationship with his wife.

Things had been fine before their marriage when Nigel had respected June's wish to remain a virgin until her wedding night. He had understood her reluctance to give her body to any man outside wedlock and that it had probably come about from her strict upbringing. There had been times during their courtship when he had got a bit carried away when they were alone. But, June had always pulled back both physically and mentally before his gentle attempts at caressing her could develop into anything passionate.

She had on many occasions wanted to confide in Nigel about her past but could never face up to telling him just what Denis Goodman had subjected her to.

That first night alone with her new husband had been far worse than June had thought possible. She'd known what was expected of her and even when Nigel showed her gentleness whilst in the throes of overdue passion, she had been capable of nothing more than closing her eyes and allowing her new husband to take her virginity, or so he thought.

How could she have ever told her new young husband that having him simply breathing heavily on her neck sent nervous shivers down her spine and just touching her in intimate places made her blood run cold. She could even smell the aroma of Lifebouy soap on his body even though she'd known it was all in her imagination. When she had looked into his soft blue eyes she didn't see his love, just the piercing evil eyes of Denis Goodman and all the old feelings of revulsion would flood her mind. She had so much hoped to have a normal sex life and be a real wife to Nigel and put all the horrors of her past behind her.

June's unwillingness to relax and enjoy their wedding night had been explained away as simple tiredness and stress of the day. Nigel accepted her excuses and reassured her everything would get better in the future. But it never did. Though June did try to feign some kind of satisfaction and interest in Nigel's lovemaking.

As a new bride, most of the few friends June had were already settled into married life and had children. Being an only child herself, she had made a promise to herself that if she were ever lucky enough to have children of her own she would like at least two.

Growing up had often been such a lonely existence. There had been many times in her young life when June would have liked an older sibling to confide in. This often turned to desperate need in her darkest hours when there was no one she trusted enough to tell of the shame and guilt she had been burdened with.

Somehow, and it was nothing less than a miracle to June, after a year of marriage she discovered she was pregnant. At first she had not given any thoughts to her "little friend's" monthly visit being a few days late. But when two weeks had passed and there had been no sign of her usual premenstrual headaches she knew there was something wrong.

43

At thirty five years old and her body clock ticking away, June had assumed she had developed women's problems rather than consider she could be pregnant. To get pregnant you had to have sex and that was something that her and Nigel had never had on a regular basis.

In the first few months of marriage the frustrated husband had tried everything he could think of to make his lovemaking efforts pleasurable, but he had accepted defeat. He resigned to the fact that June was just never going to be interested in a physical relationship. Nigel only approached her when his natural urges got the better of him and June was willing to fulfil her duty as a wife.

When a home pregnancy test had shown a very surprising positive result it had shocked June to the core. It had taken her a further two weeks before she plucked up the courage to tell Nigel their life changing news. By that time she was two months gone and was unsure of what his reaction would be but June was delighted at the prospect of parenthood. Nigel being the kind and caring man he was, accepted the news favourably though he was equally as shocked.

The couple had quickly started to feel a closeness that had been missing from their relationship and started to plan a future as a family. Then the fickle finger of fate pointed them in a different direction.

June had seen her doctor who confirmed her pregnancy. She was looking forward to her appointment at the antenatal booking clinic. Having reached the end of her first three months, her hormones had really taken hold and June had not really suffered with morning sickness. She had started to feel happier than she could ever remember.

It was at work on the November 19th 1996 when she was making one of her increasingly frequent visits to the staff toilet that June noticed a small patch of fresh blood on a sheet of toilet tissue. Looking down into the toilet pan and seeing more fresh blood had made June go weak at the knees. Somehow, she had managed to make a work colleague aware of her condition and call an ambulance.

She was never to forget the feeling of panic and desperation that consumed her in those following hours. Nigel had been by her side throughout the whole ordeal, holding her hand and trying to stay calm as he reassured her everything would be okay. But she had seen in his teary eyes that he had been as afraid as she was.

For almost six hours June was constantly monitored by doctors and nurses until a consultant obstetrician was called upon to give his opinion. After an ultrasound scan had been hastily conducted, Nigel had been quietly taken to one side and told the news they had been dreading. The scan had showed conclusively that June was having a miscarriage.

With Nigel at her bedside a young doctor had explained the urgency for June to have surgery to control the heavy bleeding and tried to reassure her she would be able to have a normal pregnancy at some time in the future. Feeling weak from the blood loss, June offered no resistance as she was hastily given a pre op injection and prepared for her trip to the operating theatre.

Waking from the deep sleep, induced by an anaesthetic, the first thought that came into June's mind was that she'd lost her baby.

The baby the couple had wanted so badly. Her morbid thoughts distracted her attention away from any physical discomfort. A nurse gave her a tablet to ease any pain she was experiencing but there was no magic pill to take away her mental agony.

The following evening June had been discharged from the hospital. Though she had been given a transfusion to rectify the effects of her heavy blood loss she'd still been physically and mentally drained. It had been thought she would be able to rest and relax better in the comforts of her own home.

Over the following couple of weeks Nigel had been wonderful as usual. He had made sure their home had been kept clean and tidy whist making sure June got the rest she needed. Neither had mentioned the miscarriage or what their future together might hold. But the closeness they had felt for a few short weeks had disappeared and they quickly reverted back to having a distant and lonely existence together. The miscarriage was never mentioned again and both knew it was unlikely June would ever be pregnant again.

When all signs of her trauma had subsided the couple were left with feeling a black cloud was hanging over them both.

June`s mother, with her prim and proper attitude to life had constantly been telling June to pull herself together and get on with life. In her tidy mind, a miscarriage was nature`s way of getting rid of something that was never meant to be. Gwen had been able to see the physical changes in her daughter caused by the pill popping habit she had developed. She hadn`t wanted June to be the brunt of any gossip and could not understand why she needed pills for depression. Gwen died in 1997 heaping even more unhappiness on her daughter when she was at her lowest ebb.

The couple stayed together for almost five more years, growing further apart as each year passed. June never returned to work after her ordeal because of her depression. Pills had been her only friends for so long that when finally weaned off them she realised Nigel had become far more distant towards her than she had imagined.

It hadn`t taken her long to suspect he was seeing another woman and when she finally plucked up the courage to confront him he made no excuses.

"I need more than you are able to give me June. To be loved in the full sense of the word. I need and I want to show my affection and be shown affection. It`s more than just sex and I doubt you will ever understand," had been Nigel`s apologetic response. "I`ve been as patient as any man could be, but the imaginary wall that that you have built around yourself is impossible to break through. What is it you are protecting yourself from June? Is it me? Just what is it?"

Even when she had been presented with a perfect opportunity to unburden her guilt and possibly save her marriage June had remained silent. She could still hear a voice inside her head saying "It`s our special little secret". The best response she could manage was to shrug her shoulders and look down at the floor.

June had known there was nothing to be gained by not giving him the chance to have a happier life with his new love and agreed to their divorce. With his new partner, Nigel moved out of the area to start a new life and June had been surprised to find the end of their marriage had been in so many ways a relief. It felt as if a great weight had been lifted from her shoulders. But yet again, she had found herself alone and had lost someone she had truly loved.

Nigel would never know the extent of the feelings June had for him and always would have. It had been because she loved him that she had let him go. She was a prisoner to her guilt and shame and it had not been fair to make her husband serve a life sentence in a one way relationship.

Now here she was again in danger of losing something she loved. She loved her job and the friends she had made. She was not going to crumble this time and have her life ruined again because of that one man. She had to take control. She would take control.

"Well not this time Denis, not this time," June uttered to herself. "It's payback time Denis and it will be our special little secret just like before."

A crafty smile broke out across June's face as she took a deep breath and felt her body starting to relax. Turning over on to her side she pulled the duvet up to her neck and nestled her head into her feather pillow.

"Let the fun begin" were her last mumbled words as she settled down again, hoping for a couple of hours more sleep which came swiftly.

Chapter 13

Tuesday 5th March 2012

June was awake before her alarm went off. This was not going to be just another Tuesday morning for her it was going to be the start of something she had often imagined but never thought it could possibly happen. It was the start of "pay-back" time. Pay back for all the years of unhappiness and loss that a certain frail old man had inflicted upon her.

The anxiety attacks she had suffered the previous day had miraculously disappeared and been replaced by a feeling of excitement and anticipation. June had awakened to a feel good factor that was a whole new experience and quite a pleasant one at that.

After a refreshing shower and two cups of coffee, it was time to let battle commence. She took one last look in the large ornate mirror that took pride of place in the hallway of her cosy flat and June was ready to make the first steps towards seeking her revenge. It would be sweet revenge by name and by nature.

That morning the short journey to Field Hall seemed to take her far less time to walk. June felt quite giddy as her heart skipped a few beats along the way. She had found herself humming one of her favourite songs as she walked with her head held high and an unfamiliar air of determination about her.

"Hey June, slow down. You're a woman on a mission this morning." June quickly turned around to see her friend Maureen trotting up alongside her. "Well you look as if you've recovered from your funny turn," she gasped, trying to keep in step with her friend.

"I'm feeling fine today. Slept well for once and ready for anything today can throw at me. I told you, it's my bloody hormones. They have a mind of their own. Yesterday I was a wreck, today I'm on top of the world," she replied grinning like the proverbial Cheshire cat.

"Good, because you really did look ill when the colour drained from your face. If men had to go through all this crap they would have found a miracle cure by now," Maureen quipped.

For the rest of the short walk to Field Hall neither of the two friends uttered another word. The silence was not in any way awkward as their friendship had allowed both women to feel comfortable in each other's company without the need for constant chatter.

June enjoyed having her best friend around her and wanted so much to confide in her about Denis Goodman and their history together. She felt sure her bosom buddy would understand and be equally as disgusted with his antics. But her friend could not be involved in what June had planned for him.

Their silence continued as they walked side by side up the front steps and into the entrance hall, passing the reception desk and into the staff quarters. As if in tune with each other's thoughts both took off their coats, placed them on their respective hooks, walked across the room together and slid their handbags into their personal lockers.

Their silence was eventually broken by Maureen who was first to enter the kitchen and was filling the kettle at the sink for their first of many brews to be made that day.

"You're very cheerful for seven thirty in the morning. Can I name that tune in one? It sounds like our cat on karaoke. Would it be Gloria Gaynor you're trying to do justice to?"

"What?"

"You're humming what sounds vaguely like...I will survive."

"I didn't realise I was. I must have heard it on the radio this morning."

"Probably. You'll be humming it all day now. But don't give up your day job."

After their brief exchange of friendly banter both checked their watches making sure they had time for their quick cuppa before starting work for the day.

Dead on 8.00am the two friends and a few other members of the team left the staff rooms for the morning's changeover meeting before starting the day's routine. Getting the residents up and out of bed, washed, dressed and ready for breakfast usually fell to the night shift. No problems had been reported and the staff disbanded.

The two friends made their way to the dining room, ready and willing to help those less able to feed themselves properly and Denis Goodman was one of the unfortunate few. Knowing that Denis would be in need of assistance June nonchalantly headed in his direction.

"Good morning Denis, did you sleep alright last night? It`s all a bit strange at first but you`ll soon settle in here. We`re all here to help."

With words of faked sincerity, June then turned towards the other new resident Ellen Gregson and asked the frail old lady the same questions. At no time could she be seen to be paying specific attention to any particular person.

If she was ever going to gain her abuser`s trust it would have to be done slowly and patiently. At no time must Denis feel he was being singled out or any of her work mates have any suspicions she had any ulterior motives for her actions. Though she had only glanced momentarily at his withered, gaunt face, his features had been burned into her memory once again. Only now she had the upper hand.

The stroke he had survived may have altered his appearance and sapped him of strength, but she knew now that she would not rest until she saw fear in his eyes. He would get to know the same fear and pain he had been happy to inflict upon his innocent victim. Soon he would be living in fear of being alone in his room waiting for his tormentor to creep in and share their "special little secret".

"Denis, you`re breakfast is going cold. Let me help you."

Picking up a fork she scooped up a dollop of scrambled egg mixed with the juice of tinned tomatoes and offered the food to the old man. June casually sat down on the dining chair next to Denis as she gently pushed the fork passed his thin lips and deposited the egg on his tongue. Before he had a chance to swallow, June had scooped up a second lot of egg and forced the fork past his lips filling his mouth.

As the third forkful of egg was being pushed into his mouth June caught a look of concern in Denis's eye's.

"C'mon darling, get it swallowed. We can't have you wasting away. Can we? Only a few more mouthfuls and you're all finished," she insisted, as a couple more heaped mouthfuls were quickly forced past his pale lips. "That's it. All done!"

She took the plate and cutlery from the table, got up from the dining chair and walked towards the waste trolley.

"Drink your tea Denis before it goes cold. I'll see you a bit later on." With a wry smile she put down the dirty plate and left the dining room happily humming a familiar tune to herself.

The day passed peacefully without any unusual events or emergencies to deal with. June had forced herself to smile at her sworn enemy every time their paths had crossed. But she made sure that he only got the same level of attention given to all the others.

At the end of their day shifts Maureen and June always walked home together or travelled by taxi when the weather was bad. Maureen lived the furthest distance away and that evening June had decided she needed to make a detour and call at the local pharmacy after she had bid goodnight to her friend.

On the short walk home Maureen spent the time chattering about her favourite soap opera and how she was looking forward to that night's episode. Not wanting to upset her companion, June mumbled the occasional "yes" or "no" whenever she felt the need to respond. Her mind was on other more pressing matters.

June just managed to get to the local pharmacy store just before the sales assistant had turned the shop sign to Closed. Realising the young girl was wanting to cash up and put the lock on the door, she apologised for being so late in calling and quickly picked an item from the display shelves. Satisfied that she had got her purchase she thanked the assistant and set off on the short walk back to her flat.

What a difference a day makes or so the song goes. Just twenty four hours earlier it had been a different woman who had collapsed in a heap, drained of her strength and ability to think rationally.

That night it was a woman full of determination, revenge and pure hatred that entered the ground floor apartment that had become her much loved home.

After flicking the switch on the kettle for a refreshing cup of tea, June took out the contents of the flimsy white plastic carrier bag. She placed it on the shiny black onyx work surface which complemented her Beech wood kitchen cupboards.

Her purchase was a bottle of an old medicinal product, not often used today but June knew exactly what she would be using it for and the effects it could cause. At least two other items were needed for the task she had in mind and she was almost certain that one of the objects could be found lurking in the back of her wardrobe or in one of the matching set of drawers. She would hunt it out after her tea. She had something more pressing to do first.

With a mug of hot tea and a couple of chocolate digestive biscuits on a tray June lowered her body onto the cool leather seat cushions of her sofa. She looked across the room and glanced at her laptop on the carpet. It had been on charge all day so it would be ready for her to search the internet for the last of the items she needed.

"I knew you would come in useful to me one day and today`s the day," she said out loud.

The laptop had been bought under some duress the previous year. Maureen and a few of the other girls at work had insisted June drag herself into the twenty first century and buy a computer. After much persuasion she had agreed to sign up to a broadband provider. Apart from being able to communicate with her friends via Facebook and sending an occasional email, the laptop had been used mainly for playing games. A scrabble style game in particular had kept June and Maureen pitting their vocabulary knowledge against each other for months. That night she was to search the internet for a few specific items that if she wanted to purchase would be delivered to her door and would not arouse suspicion from a shop assistant. The sale of one such item in a shop would most certainly have caused a few raised eyebrows.

It didn`t take long to search Amazon for the required items and place her order. Delivery would take a couple of days. That was just perfect timing for June as she needed to think carefully through her plans.

That evening, unlike the previous one, June spent feeling calm and relaxed and having regained her appetite, a microwaveable ready meal had been enjoyed. She even managed to concentrate on a couple of episodes of Maureen's favourite soap operas. At least she would be able to contribute to the conversations that would surely be taking place the following day.

Turning off all the lights and switches for the night, June picked up the carrier bag with her purchase and took it to her bedroom. Handling the item before placing them into the back of her underwear drawer brought another wry smile to her face.

"Oh Denis, what fun we are going to have. Let's see how much you enjoy sharing this special little secret," she laughed.

Chapter 14

Just as June had expected, Maureen was bubbling over with enthusiasm about the previous night`s television dramas as they walked to work the following morning. Humouring her dear friend, she joined in to discuss the villains of the current plots. For the next few days all she had to do was behave normally. Then her plans could be put into action.

Their working day started out in much the normal way. The morning meeting was uneventful with the supervisor of the night staff updating the day shift of any problems or concerns that had developed through the night.

It had been noted that their new male resident had particularly bad speech problems. His stroke had left him only able to make grunting and groaning noises, so all staff had to be aware of his problem. Extra care and patience would be needed to help him communicate his needs. A communal response of nodding heads from the staff meant everyone would do their best to help the poor unfortunate man.

Unfortunate for you Denis, but very fortunate for me, was the thought that passed through June`s mind followed by, *Very fortunate!*

The morning routines had gone smoothly. At lunchtime most of the residents were seated in the dining room and those able to feed themselves were tucking into their plates of sausage, mashed potato and peas. Those less fortunate, which included Denis Goodman, were awaiting assistance from the staff. It was an opportunity too good to pass up. June quickly seized the chance to sit next to him.

Trying to ignore her compulsive urge to smash his head into the plate of food, she took a deep breath and picked up a fork. A thought flashed through her brain at the speed of light, but the idea was contained. Stabbing him in the neck would be too obvious and she wanted him to suffer before he went to meet his maker. If there was any justice to be had he would go straight to hell.

"C'mon Denis let me help you with your lunch. We can't have you wasting away can we? Do you like sausages Denis?"

His only response was a simple nodding of the head and a throaty groan.

"Can't you speak at all Denis?"

Again he responded with a slow shaking of the head.

"What about your left arm? You can use that can't you?"

This time he managed a facial expression that was somewhere between a snarl and a frown.

"Well, you're going to need a lot of help from us so let's start with getting you fed."

June started shovelling food past his drooping bottom lip and into his mouth. Each forkful she fed him was getting bigger as she used every ounce of self-control not to ram the fork to the back of his throat, putting an end to his miserable life. It was only when he started to splutter and cough out a dollop of mashed potato that she regained her composure. *Not yet June. Not yet,* she reminded herself.

After asking him if he had eaten enough of his lunch, June picked up the wasted plate of food and placed it on the trolley alongside all the other dirty plates.

"Would you like a cup of tea Denis? Do you take sugar?"

He nodded his head in reply and June poured half a cup of tea from the urn, adding milk and sugar before taking it over to him.

"Now Denis, let's see if you can grasp this cup. If not we'll have to get you a special mug. That's it. Now try to raise it to your mouth. Try a bit higher. No, it's too heavy for you. Here, I'll hold the cup and you try to sip your tea."

After a couple of attempts to take a drink from the cup Denis made one of his groaning noises which indicated he wanted to stop.

"I'll try and sort out a caring cup for you. This is not going to work." June took the cup back to the trolley.

"Are you ready to go back into the day room Denis?"

He nodded. With that signal she moved the table to one side and braced herself to touch him. Holding out her arm for him to grasp,

55

she again supressed an overwhelming urge to grab his neck and squeeze the life out of him.

Slowly he raised his frail body, grasping her arm as tightly as he could with his left hand. When he was finally standing as upright as he possibly could June helped him to get seated in his wheelchair and then began to push it on their short journey to the television room.

Those few seconds that passed had been a challenge to keep control of her actions. Having him touch her had made her skin creep but it would all be worth it in the end.

Having got Denis settled into one of the numerous high seat chairs, June made a much needed visit to the staff toilets. The need to relieve her full bladder was an additional benefit to come from the few minutes of solitude she sought in the locked cubicle. Gaining her composure to continue with the rest of day`s work had been the objective. If she was to carry out her intended plans it was imperative her prey should feel at ease in her care. With that thought she took a couple of deep breaths before unlocking the cubicle door. Determined to give as much attention to all the other residents and allay any suspicions, June spent the rest of her day displaying her usual cheery persona.

Chapter 15

Thursday 7th March 2012

Thursday morning dawned and it was more than the sun that was an early riser. June had slept quite well after spending a relaxing evening and preparing a few things to take in to work with her. Her purchases from Amazon had arrived the previous day. She had carefully placed a couple of items into the pockets of her blue tunic. With a few surprises in store for Denis it was only a matter of waiting for an opportunity to present itself.

After their usual walk to work with Maureen, eagerly updating her friend on the turbulent love life of her eldest son and how her middle son was doing so well in the police force. June was a little slower than usual at removing her coat and putting her bag into her locker. She needed to make sure the contents of her tunic pocket were securely in place and not visible to the eye. Maureen didn`t notice her friends hesitation as she was still rambling on about her son`s cheating lover.

June slid her hand inside her pocket for a final check. Nothing had moved so she removed her coat and finally was able to stop her friend`s constant chatter by saying, "Right, let`s get that kettle on."

At the morning meeting there had been nothing of any interest to report. It had been a run of the mill night, but a member of the night staff had been taken ill. Cover would be required for a couple of nights and a request for a volunteer to swap shifts had been made.

June had previously worked night shifts, but for the past five years both she and Maureen had worked regular day shifts. Without hesitation she raised her hand gesturing she was volunteering.

Maureen flashed a look of complete surprise at her friend.

Shrugging her shoulders she whispered, "What? I just thought it would be a change."

What she failed to disclose was the opportunity to be alone with a certain person was too good to miss. Events were working in June's favour for once.

Instead of being just another working day it was going to be an eventful night for someone at least. June had gone back home after the morning meeting to get some rest before returning to work through the night. She knew rest would not come easily to her with her adrenal glands working overtime.

Before trying to have an afternoon nap she needed to prepare a few things in addition to the items that were already in her tunic's pocket. Once she had run through her plans in her head, all she had to do was wait for the right moment to strike on her unsuspecting target.

Residents at Field Hall had no set bed times. It was up to each individual what time they chose to retire each night. The more active of them liked to sit in the television lounge and watch Coronation Street, Emmerdale and Eastenders with their friends, chatting about the goings on in each programme. The less fortunate ones, some suffering from the early stages of dementia had very little interest in television or forming friendships. These residents were usually the first to be helped prepare for bed and be safely tucked in for the night.

Denis Goodman was unlikely to taking part in any discussions with his speech being impaired so badly so he would probably be one of the first to be attended to. At least that is what June was hoping for. She was going to make sure she was readily available when her favourite resident required some assistance. That was her mission for the night. She mulled over her plans whilst making the short walk to work.

Her shift started at seven o'clock and though she had only managed a couple of hours dozing on her sofa that afternoon she was feeling quite perky. For the second time that day June carefully checked the contents of her tunic pocket before taking off her coat and locking up her bag.

She exchanged pleasantries with the other ladies, some she had got to know very well from her years of working nights. Apart from meeting briefly at the end of a shift, June had not really had much contact with her old work mates but there was no awkwardness when they all headed off to get a quick cup of coffee.

In the few minutes they spent together in the staff kitchen she was quickly brought up to speed on the routine and any changes that had been implemented since her last spell of night duty. Any anxiety she may have been feeling had nothing to do with the work schedule, but if her colleagues wished to think it that was fine by her.

About an hour into her shift June had assisted in putting a couple of the residents to bed. These two had little mobility but were happy to watch television from the comfort of their own beds. Each room had a flat screen television mounted on a wall with a remote pad enabling them to control their own viewing choices. So unless they needed to press their emergency buttons it would be a couple of hours before they needed checking again. June decided to go check on who was in the television lounge and immediately on entry she clocked Denis sat in the far corner of the room. He was alone, isolated from the other residents.

A few of the old ladies were discussing the episode of Eastenders that they had just watched and were oblivious to June speaking to Denis.

"Are you okay? Don`t you like the soaps Denis? If you`re tired I can help you turn in."

She looked directly into his eyes for any sign of a response. Nothing had changed. His eyes still showed no signs of any emotion and it still disturbed June to look into them. But he surprised her by making mumbling noises as if trying to tell her something.

"Do you want to go to bed Denis? Nod if you do. Is this your wheelchair?"

He managed a slow nodding movement. She stood up and reached for the handles of his wheelchair which had been left close by and manoeuvred it to the front of him. He had used a chair the previous day so she assumed he must be feeling very weak.

"Right, Grab my arm and we`ll take it slowly. That`s it, nice and steady does it," she grimaced as her skin crawled at his touch. He held her arm tightly with his left hand as she assisted him into the wheelchair.

Her heart skipped a beat as the couple slowly left the lounge and made their way across the hall towards his room. June slid her hand into her pocket feeling the contents that she had carefully placed in readiness for such an opportunity.

Denis's room was situated on the ground floor in the newest part of the building which had been added onto the Hall some years earlier. Once inside his room and the brakes of the wheelchair had been firmly pulled on, she braced herself again to have him touch her. She closed his room door, drew a deep breath and turned to face him.

He had managed to stand up from his wheelchair with June's help and shuffled towards his en suite bathroom. Only when he had got close to the toilet pan did she remove his left hand from her arm. She placed it onto a grab rail attached to the left of the tiled wall which was specifically placed to assist residents with their mobility.

June returned to close the bathroom door and took the opportunity to remove a latex glove from her pocket.

"I'll help you with your zip Denis. You keep hold of the rail and you won't lose your balance."

She slipped her right hand smoothly into the surgical glove then pulled out a very small plastic bag from her pocket. Holding the small bag with her left hand she placed her gloved hand inside the bag and moved it as if trying to grasp some flimsy contents. Quickly removing her hand from the bag she returned it to her pocket and turned towards Denis.

Standing behind the man she loathed, she reached out with her latex covered hand to feel for the zip in his trousers. Slowly she pulled the zip down as far as it would go. Bracing herself, she pushed her hand inside the gaping hole and fumbled inside his underpants. Grasping the limp lump of flesh she pulled it quickly and firmly out of his trousers, exposing his shrivelled genitalia. With gritted teeth she kept hold of his penis and pointed it downwards and towards the toilet pan.

"There you go Denis. Nothing to be embarrassed about is there?" she said supressing the urge to be sick. Before she had finished speaking he had already started to spray urine into the pan.

Waiting for him to empty his bladder seemed to take an eternity but eventually the dribbles stopped. Now was her chance to act.

Letting his penis flop she quickly slid her hand back inside her tunic pocket and fumbled with the small plastic bag again. Then her gloved hand moved swiftly from her pocket and grasped his penis with a very firm grip.

She started to move her tightly closed fist up and down pushing back the wizened foreskin whilst rubbing her thumb over the exposed tip. Then very faintly she whispered into his ear, "This can be our special little secret Denis. You like keeping secrets don`t you Denis?"

He made a throaty groaning noise as June tightened her grip and pulled at the flaccid flesh even harder. She felt him wobble as he lost his hold on the rail. Hastily, she rammed his penis back inside his trousers. Pulled up his zip and whispered in his ear again, "Did you like that Denis?"

Quickly removing her latex glove and stuffing it back in her pocket she moved to his left side and placed his hand onto her arm.

"Right, let`s get you into bed."

Making sure she didn`t look the frail old man in the eye at any time, she helped him make the few steps to his bed where he flopped down onto the mattress. Though his walking resembled more of a shuffling of his feet, June could sense the effect her actions had on his body. He was more unstable than he had been before their visit to the bathroom.

She had him just where she wanted him. If he was upset at her vulgar fondling of his genitals that was good, because it was only the start of what she had in mind for him. It was the start of "pay- back" time.

Denis sat on the edge of his bed while June went back to close the bathroom door. She spotted the remote pad for the television was on the bedside cabinet and walked over to pick it up and press the "On" button.

Flat screen televisions were mounted on the walls of every room to free up more space for any special mobility aids that each resident may need. Denis`s room was equipped with a basic brown tubular framed commode, a tripod based walking stick as well as a wheelchair.

"Right, let`s get you undressed."

Still avoiding eye contact she removed his clothing very slowly, folding each item neatly. His cotton pyjamas were at hand on the bottom of his bed and helping him on with them meant June having to touch his bare flesh again. She braced herself once more and slowly helped him dress for bed.

"Now Denis, stand up for a second and I`ll pull back the sheets." With her assistance he managed to stand and was gripping her arm again.

"Right, sit down and I`ll help you swing your legs up."

He did as requested and June was able to lift his thin spindly legs up onto the bed.

"Right, are you going to watch a bit of television or shall I turn it off?"

He responded by raising his left hand and waiving it very slowly.

"You want it turned off then. Now are you comfy Denis?"

She pulled the sheets up to his chest. "Right, I`ve just one more thing to do and then I`ll let you rest."

Staring him directly in the eyes, June slid her right hand into her pocket once again. She pulled her hand out of her pocket and with her left hand grabbed Denis firmly by the chin and pulled down his bottom lip forcing his mouth open.

Before he had a chance to make a sound she forced a syringe into his mouth and plunged the entire contents into the back of his throat. As her left hand forced his jaw upwards and his mouth to close, June moved her face up close to his and whispered in his ear. "Swallow that you bastard. There`s plenty more to come."

She waited until she was sure he had swallowed the liquid before relaxing her grip on his chin and moved her face even closer to his. She whispered, "Do you remember our little secret Denis? I do. Sweet dreams."

June turned off the television and made a hasty exit from his room.

As she walked slowly back down the corridor she pulled open her pocket and looked down at the contents. She needed to dispose of the latex glove covered in powder and the empty syringe. How would she explain having a bag of itching powder and a syringe with traces of syrup of figs in her pocket?

She paid a hasty visit to the staff room and opened her locker. Quickly opening her handbag she scooped the incriminating evidence out of her pocket and dropped it inside and zipped it up. It was mission accomplished for the time being.

No matter how hard the old man swallowed, the sour taste remained on his tongue. It wasn't a taste he was familiar with and certainly not his usual medication. He was feeling confused at the strange behaviour June had displayed towards him. His genitals were feeling hot and itchy. He tried to relieve the constant irritation by scratching his penis with his left hand but the itching continued and his groin area was starting to feel sore.

Why was this woman saying things to him that he did not understand? What had she done to him? Those were the only thoughts that filled his confused brain as he continued to scratch and scratch and scratch.

Chapter 16

Throughout the night June had been expecting fatigue to creep up on her with not having had a decent sleep before she reported for night duty. Surprisingly, she felt anything but tired and was feeling quite bubbly and enjoying her time working alongside her old workmates. Between the usual bedtime routines she had been able to catch up on the gossip about her colleague`s domestic trials and tribulations.

One question that had been asked more than once that evening was directly aimed at June. Everyone wanted to know if she had got herself a new man in her life. With a smile and a "not likely", said in a light hearted manner, everyone seemed to accept her answer and think no more about it.

It was a little after midnight when she heard the familiar tone of an alarm buzzer echoing through the first corridor. Each resident had an alarm button beside their bed which they could use to summon for help.

June had been in the second corridor helping a chap pay a visit to the toilet. She and a couple of other women ran to the reception entrance to look at the board placed upon the wall. The board had just one flashing light and on looking up June could see it was the resident of room number five that had pressed the panic button. Room five was Denis Goodman`s room.

June would normally have been quick off the mark to respond to anyone`s alarm going off but hesitated as her head started to spin. To her great relief the other two women dashed off to room five without noticing her slow reactions. She took a few deep breaths to steady her nerves and clear her head then returned to the task she had been forced to break off from. She needed to appear as relaxed as possible when her colleagues Rita Kemp and Freda Redfern returned from the alarm call.

It had been almost twenty minutes before the pair returned.

"My god, what is it with men? From their cradle to their grave they just can't stop fiddling with their bits. He's rubbed it till it's red raw. He's a randy old bugger," were the less than compassionate words of Rita.

"For a one armed man he's given it a good polish," retorted Freda with a laugh.

"What's happened?" June asked in as casual way, hoping she sounded genuinely interested

"That new chap Denis, he's only got the use of his left arm but managed to wank himself 'til he's as sore as hell. He's mumbling something I can't understand and holding his tackle to show me. I do hope he wasn't wanting me to have a go with it. Didn't look as if he'd hit the jackpot either because there wasn't any wet bits," Rita explained with a hint of lewd sarcasm.

"What have you done then?" enquired June.

"Not much we could do except give it a wash it with a cold flannel to cool it down and hope it stops him fiddling with it. Told him to leave it alone and we'll get the nurse to look at it in the morning. Perhaps she should get him something to dampen his urges"

"That's men for you" June replied smiling, "it's always sex, sex, sex!"

The rest of the shift passed without any more problems or alarms. The hours seemed to fly by for June who had spent most of the time checking and assisting with the less mobile to be turned in their beds every couple of hours. On the few occasions that June had not been concentrating on the needs of the residents, her mind had drifted back to Denis and her actions towards him.

What could she do next to make him feel revulsion and humiliated? She knew what she really wanted was to see him dead but not before she had seen fear in his eyes and heard him begging her for forgiveness. But, she knew her actions would have to be carefully planned and executed. Another idea had already popped into her head and she would be able to work on it when she finished her shift.

June sighed as she turned the key in the lock and opened the door to her apartment. Finally the energy that had kept her so bright and bubbly throughout the night had diminished and been replaced by a sense of relief and fatigue. Kicking off her shoes in the small entrance hall and hanging up her coat, she walked straight towards the sofa and picked up the television remote control. A cup of coffee and a catch up on the national news headlines was what she needed to relax before taking to her bed for a few hours.

Chapter 17

"Why can't I stay on my own? I'll be okay if the doors are locked. I promise I will stay in my room. Please, please let me. I don't want anyone to babysit. I'm almost a teenager!"

June's pleading had gone on for almost an hour. But Gwen Sweet was determined her daughter was not going to stay in their home alone while they attended the annual New Year's Eve party thrown by Herbert's employers.

"June, you are eleven, not a teenager and Uncle Denis is coming round to stay with you as he always does on New Year's Eve. Now stop going on about it. He will be here soon," were Gwen's final words on the subject.

June began to feel sick when she heard voices in the hallway. His familiar voice made the blood run cold through her young body. Her feet felt as if they are glued to the floor; her legs too weak to run. She didn't want to see his face, hear his voice or smell his scent. He always smelled of Lifebuoy soap and just a small whiff of that familiar fragrance caused her to feel instantly queasy.

Gwen was closely followed by her brother as she returned to the living room where June stood feeling helpless and panic stricken. She could instantly smell him as he casually walked towards her and attempted to place a kiss on her forehead. She froze as he began to speak.

"And how's my favourite niece? I missed you at Christmas dear. Are you feeling better now? Did you like your bracelet?"

She gave him no reply.

"June. What is the matter with you today? Say thank you for your present. Denis, she has been in a funny mood for days. I'm not sure she is fully recovered. Maybe I should take her to see the doctor. Anyway we have to be off now. We should be back a little after midnight."

Herbert Sweet entered the room whilst buttoning up his tweed overcoat.

"Hello Denis. Help yourself to a drink, you know where it is. There's a few bottles of beer in the fridge as well. Right, we need to be off. Our meal is being served at seven thirty sharp."

Both Herbert and Gwen placed kisses on June's forehead and headed out of the room. The sound of the front door closing brought about a feeling of helplessness. There was nowhere to escape even if she had found the strength to do so. Feeling rooted to the spot she tried to avert his leering dark brown eyes.

"Now my dear, come and sit next to me on the sofa. What would you like to watch on television?" he said as he reached for her left hand and tried to coax her towards him. With her legs trembling she was unable to offer an ounce of resistance.

Her head was feeling woozy as she sat beside him and every bit of strength had drained from her body. She could hear him speaking but his words did not register. He continued speaking while gently rubbing his thumb over the back of her hand.

"Come closer my dear. You do look under the weather. Let Uncle Denis give you a cuddle and make you feel better."

He edged his body closer to hers and his right arm snaked across her shoulders, drawings her body closer to him in the familiar way she has come to dread.

For a time he appeared to be interested in watching the television and his eyes were transfixed on the screen. He continued to gently rub his thumb across the back of her hand. She sat rigid waiting for him to turn his attention back to her and eventually he did.

"Now dear, what on earth has been wrong with you? Do you still feel ill? Come here let Uncle Denis make you feel better. You know how to make Uncle Denis feel better don't you?"

As the dreaded words flowed from his mouth he released her hand and wrapped his left arm around her, squeezing her with both arms. She felt a tightening in her throat as his hand slid up to her chest and cupped her right breast. He started fondling her, rubbing his fingers over the thin fabric of the pyjama top she was wearing.

His hand slithered down to her waist. His probing fingers lifted up the hem of her top and started to explore her naked belly until finally pushing his hand further up and again he grasped her naked, small breast.

Nuzzling his head into the nape of her neck she could feel his hot breath on her skin. It stank of whisky. Her father's breath often had the same smell when he kissed her goodnight.

His breathing started to get faster and he began making the familiar moaning sounds as he continued to fondle each breast. She felt pain as his fingers pinched her small developing nipples. The smell of Lifebouy overpowered her senses.

As he kissed her neck he whispered "You are so pretty my dear. You make Uncle Denis so very happy. You're such a good girl. You like to make me happy don't you? This is our special little secret."

Bracing herself for what she thought was to happen, June put up no defence and fought back the urge to vomit.

He stopped and removed his left hand from inside her top. His right arm moved away from her shoulders as he turned his attention to the waistband of her pyjama bottoms. He pushed his hand down to feel the contours of her pubic area. His fingers roughly probed her flesh causing her to tense her thigh muscles. He removed his hand and seized her by the waist and used both his hands to pull his victim down so she is almost lying flat on the cushions of the sofa. Tugging at the elasticated waistband of her pyjama's, he managed to pull them down to the top of her thighs. She was still unable to put up a fight as panic swept over her.

Again he stopped and turned his attention to his own trousers, hastily unbuttoning the waistband and pulled down his zip. Within a second he had freed his engorged penis. June tried to avert her eyes but was unable to stop herself from looking at the repulsive sight of his male genitalia.

His movements became more aggressive as he began again to pull down her nightwear and drag them past her knees. He looked at June and she saw the all too familiar piercing look in his evil eyes. His face was puce and he looked angry as his breathing got even faster and louder.

Her mind went blank as she closed her eyes. She felt his body on top of her, crushing her against the cushions of the sofa. He forced her legs apart with his hands. Unable to breathe properly her head started to spin as he forced all his weight upon her. She felt pressure in her groin and a sharp pain. Then, more pain as he continued lifting his body and forcing himself even harder and faster inside her.

Her uncle`s face was next to hers. Grunting and saying her name over and over she was aware of him repeatedly pushing something inside her causing the pain she was feeling. As his pushing became more aggressive her pain got stronger until she felt a hot sensation inside her. He moaned out loud as his body collapsed onto hers. For a few seconds he didn`t move or speak. June wondered if he had died. Then he lifted himself up off her body and pulled away. She was aware of something hot running down her inner thigh.

"Now, there`s no need to worry dear, I won`t tell your mother what you have just done. It`s just our secret. You`re my special girl. Now go clean yourself up and we`ll watch some television when you come back," he whispered to her as he stuffed his deflated penis back into his trousers.

The young girl slowly raised herself up from the sofa and made her way towards the living room door. Her rapist relaxed back into the sofa`s cushions, enjoying the afterglow of fulfilling his sexual fantasy.

Chapter 18

June sat bolt upright in her bed. She brushed her right hand across her face and wiped away a few beads of cold sweat from her top lip. Her cotton pyjamas felt damp to the touch. Her shaking hand immediately moved to her groin. She could feel pain.

Taking a few seconds to clear her head she rubbed her bleary eyes. Then the realisation hit her that she had only been dreaming.

It had been years since she had last had that disturbing dream. It had been buried away in the darkest recess of her mind or so she had thought. Now it was back. Denis Goodman had raped her on that New Year's Eve in her own home and now it felt as if he had done it all over again. All the familiar feelings of shame swept over her taking her back to a place she had fought so long to get out of.

Wide awake and with not a chance of getting back to sleep June pushed back the duvet and kicked her legs over the side of her bed. Even though she knew it had all been a bad dream she was still cupping her groin with her right hand, checking for traces of any hot semen or blood. The sensation felt so real.

Anger was turning to blind rage as she stood up and walked over to the bedroom door and reached for her favourite pink towelling bath robe, kept hanging from a hook on the door. As she slipped her arms into the sleeves and wrapped the robe around her body, the softness of the fabric and smell of fragrant detergent gave her some comfort as the gown encased her body. Closing her eyes June took a deep breath. Her mind was in turmoil but she knew one thing was certain. Denis Goodman was going to pay for his sins and it was going to be a pleasure making sure he got his just desserts.

The last minutes of sunlight were fading as June opened the kitchen blinds and reached for the kettle. A quick glance at her watch told her it was almost 3.30pm. She had only managed a few hours of sleep and was feeling drained of energy. A lack of sleep she could cope with but dreaming about her last encounter with her rapist had sent shockwaves through her body once again.

June made her way back from the kitchen, through to the lounge, and flopped down onto one of her brown faux leather dining chairs. She slumped across the glass topped dining table. Staring into a cup of steaming coffee, she was still trying to put the sickening thoughts to the back of her mind and surprised herself with a sudden outburst of, "Fucking evil bastard!" pouring freely from her mouth.

Never before had she used common gutter language, as her late mother had called it, but today the words had not only seemed appropriate but had slipped off her tongue so easily.

"Fuck you Denis! Fuck, fuck, fuck, fuck, fuck you!" Just saying the forbidden words brought her a small amount of satisfaction.

After taking a large gulp of coffee she drew a deep breath, flexed her shoulders and exhaled slowly. She had preparations to make before her next shift started, just a few hours away.

After a second cup of coffee and an invigorating hot shower June felt wide awake and much calmer in mind. With her hair washed and carefully wrapped in a towel, she massaged her favourite body lotion into skin still tingling from the fierce spray of hot water. Now the pain in her groin that she was feeling was very real. An urge to vigorously scrub her entire genital area and wash away all traces of imaginary semen had left her skin raw.

After blow drying her hair and getting dressed, June felt a sense of calmness in both mind and body. She needed a clear head if she was going to deal with her Nemesis later that night.

At the bottom of her handbag lay the syringe which had been hastily hidden after administering Denis with a large dose of syrup of figs. Underneath laid the latex glove she had used to give his penis a thorough covering with itching powder.

"Thank you Amazon," June said out loud as she scooped up the incriminating evidence and dropped it into her kitchen waste bin. The laptop that she had been urged to buy had finally been put to some constructive use when she made her recent purchases on line.

She picked up her handbag and carried it back into the lounge, placed it on the carpet next to the sofa and walked back to her bedroom. She headed towards the set of pine drawers in the far corner of the room. Slowly she pulled open the top drawer she used for storing her underwear. Tights, briefs and bra's filled the entire space, but she pushed her hand to the back of the drawer and pulled out a box of latex gloves. A second dip into the colourful display of lace and cotton garments and out popped another package which contained syringes.

It had been easy to buy syringes without needles as they were commonly used to administer medicines to animals by mouth. Buying on line had meant no one would question her purchases. Another syringe and a glove were taken from the boxes which she carefully returned to the back of the drawer.

Back in the privacy of her kitchen, June was able to continue her skull duggery. She reached up to the back of a small cupboard where a varied collection of herbs and spices were neatly kept. June's hand moved the jars to one side and grasped a paper bag. Very carefully the bag was placed onto the work surface.

A quick rummage in one of the drawers and she produced a couple of small unused plastic bags. Now she had all that was needed for preparing her next little surprise for Denis Goodman.

The powdery contents had to be handled with care and June had already slipped her right hand into a glove before opening up the bag. Making sure none spilled out she poured a small amount of the powder into one of the plastic bags then carefully folded over the top of it to keep the any from escaping.

Removing the glove without any powder coming into contact with her skin was a delicate manoeuvre but it was easily done. The paper bag that contained the itching powder was returned to the hiding place at the back of the cupboard.

From another cupboard June reached for a glass tumbler and partially filled it with cold water. Then, clutching a plastic container grabbed from another small cupboard, she poured some of the contents into the water. The white grainy substance dissolved instantly. She placed the container back in the cupboard with the label forward facing. The label was marked Salt.

June picked up the new syringe and pushed the plunger down to the bottom as she dipped the tip into the salt solution. Drawing the plunger slowly up the syringe filled up and she placed it in the remaining plastic bag.

June sighed deeply as she gazed out of the kitchen window. The afternoon sunlight had been replaced with a velvet blue sky. As she reached for the cord to pull down the off white roller blind, her eyes were drawn to a corner of the window sill. In the bottom left corner a spider was spinning a web.

Spiders in the home had never been a problem to June but watching that particular one dangling from its delicate web brought back memories of her mother and the dreadful phobia she had suffered.

Gwen Sweet had never been able to stand the sight of even the smallest spider and would flee the house if she caught even a glimpse of one. It had always fallen to June or her father to trap the poor creatures under a glass tumbler and deposit them outside. Only when Gwen was reassured her home was spider free would she step back indoors. Occasionally, if Herbert had been in a mischievous mood he would pretend to have a spider in his hand and chase his panic stricken wife around their home.

June was smiling at the fond memories of her parents when a sudden thought dawned on her. Her uncle had also had a phobia about spiders and it had not just been spiders he had thoroughly hated. He had despised hypodermic needles even more. His fear of needles had made him reluctant to visit a dentist for fear of needing an injection and his teeth had paid the price. His smile was anything but perfect due to a couple of prominent broken molars.

"Oh, thank you God. Thank you," she said aloud as a big smile spread across her face. Whilst unable to resist smirking from ear to ear, a tumbler was hastily taken from a cupboard and the unsuspecting spider was captured within it.

"Now my little, long legged friend, you and I have a date to keep."

Chapter 19

Feeling extremely pleased with herself June had been looking forward to working her night shift. She had made sure that her colleagues had left the staff cloakroom before opening her locker and placing her handbag inside it. Once she knew there were no prying eyes to see her actions, the zip of her black leather bag was opened and she started to transfer some of the contents into her blue tunic pocket.

The first item was a small clear cylindrical container with a white screw top. The nursing staff had a large supply of these little pots which were used for sending patient's urine specimens for analysis. June had taken a few pots home some months ago when she had suspected she may have cystitis.

The content of the pot she was holding in her hand was anything but urine. Trying to scramble up the inside of the pot was the long legged spider she had taken from her kitchen window sill.

The next object to be transferred was the syringe full of salt water. Making sure the liquid had not leaked out June reached for the latex glove and the bag of itching powder. With her bag zipped, locker door secured and a reassuring check of the contents in her pocket, June left the cloakroom to join the rest of the staff.

At the usual meeting held before every change of shift, a run through of any problems that had occurred or needed the staff's urgent attention was been gone through. There had been nothing unusual reported until Denis Goodman's name was mentioned. June's ears had pricked up and she'd braced herself for what was to be said.

"Severe irritation, genital area and loose bowels," were mentioned by a couple of the staff members. June could feel her pulse racing and her head spinning a little as she tried to digest what was being said.

Denis had not wanted to leave his room throughout the day and everyone had been asked to keep him under regular observation. As he had only been a resident for a few days, staff members had not yet been able to understand his mumblings. There were a few other residents who had speech impediments due to the effects of having had a stroke, but after a while their distorted attempts at conversation became understandable. Denis was not able to make himself clearly understood and that suited June just fine.

The first couple of hours of the shift passed uneventful with residents being helped to get ready for bed whenever they chose to retire for the night. June was in a constant state of alert just biding her time until she could pay a secret visit to her uncle.

A few minutes past 11.00pm, June was due to take the first of her fifteen minute breaks. She intended to put the time to good use.

"Right Freda, I'll take my break now while it's all quiet on the home front. Shall I look in on poor Denis and see if he's okay first?"

"Yes do. He may be asleep but better be sure he's okay," was the reply June had hoped for from her colleague.

"Back in a bit then."

She set off at a casual walking pace, headed down the first corridor and stopped outside room number five. She drew a deep breath and exhaled slowly as her hand grabbed the door handle. Slowly she turned the handle and pushed the door open just far enough to be able to peer inside the room.

"Hello Denis. How are you feeling?" she whispered. "I've heard that you've not been feeling well."

She closed the door behind her as quietly as possible and walked over to his bed.

"Oh, Denis. What are we going to do with you? Been scratching your private parts I hear. Let's see what's going on down there."

She slid her right hand into her tunic pocket and pulled out the latex glove. The glove was easily slipped onto her hand and she reached into her pocket again for the small plastic bag. Hastily, the gloved hand was dipped into the bag of itching powder and the latex fingers covered with the irritating substance.

June's movements were swift and within seconds she had pulled back Denis's bed sheets and yanked down the front of his pyjama bottoms.

"Not much to brag about down there, is there Denis? It looks more like a dead slug than a penis," she sneered.

As quick as a flash, her gloved hand had mauled his testicles and grabbed the "dead slug". Rubbing her hand up and down, she made sure as much of the flaccid flesh was covered with the itching powder.

She wasted no time in throwing back the sheets to cover his frail body and pulling off the latex glove. As she placed the glove back in her pocket her hand grabbed one of the syringes.

June put her right knee on the bed and held down Denis's left arm. Forcing his jaw to open with her left hand she forced the syringe full of salt water down the back of his throat.

"Swallow it!" she said angrily as her left hand clamped his mouth shut.

Her victim feebly moved his head from side to side trying to avoid swallowing.

"I said swallow didn't I? So fucking swallow it!" With her anger rising, her right hand pinched his nose. He swallowed, almost choking as he did.

Within seconds June had the other syringe in her hand and repeated the process. He was forced to swallow the syrup of figs. When his spluttering had ceased she put her hand over his mouth again and in a haunting whisper said, "I've got another little surprise for you Denis. I've brought a little friend to see you."

She took the small container out of her pocket and held it up to his contorted face.

"It's a spider Denis. I know how much you like spiders. Would you like me to leave him to keep you company? I could put him down your pyjamas or maybe let him sleep in the bed with you. Would you like that Denis? Or should I just let him crawl all over your miserable face?"

The old man's face had turned grey and his expression was one of sheer terror.

77

"Don`t you fucking dare peg out on me you fucking pervert. I`ve got lots of surprises in store for you. Do you know why? Has the fucking penny dropped yet you perverted lump of shite? It will. I`ll keep the spider for now," she taunted in a chilling manner as she lifted her knee from his arm and took a step back. The container complete with spider was put back into her pocket.

"Sleep tight and don`t you dare forget. This is our special little secret Denis. Just ours and only ours. Do you understand Denis?"

His watery brown eyes looked directly into his tormentor`s and she could see his fear as a tear ran down his cheek.

"Are you afraid of me Denis? Well so you should be. Why do I want to hurt you? Well that gives you something to think about until we meet again."

June turned around and walked towards the door. Before she stepped out into the corridor she turned to glance one more time at the frail and frightened shell of an old man.

"Just buzz if you need anything Denis. Goodnight," she said in her usual friendly manner, aware that if anyone heard her leaving room number five they would not have their suspicions aroused. All she had to do before taking her break was dispose of the evidence stuffed in her pocket.

After a quick visit to the cloakroom to deposit the empty syringes in her handbag and release her long legged friend from the container, June headed off to make herself a cup of coffee.

Delighted to find the staff room empty she was able to flop into a comfy armchair and reflect on her actions.

Her heart was still racing from the fear of being caught in the act. Her head was full of mixed emotions. Hatred and exhilaration were battling head on for dominance in her confused brain. Exhilaration became the outright winner. As much as she feared being caught and losing her job, the strange sensation of having the power to hurt Denis was one of great satisfaction. She finally felt he imaginary chains that had bound her for decades were beginning to weaken. The worm had turned.

Feeling calmer and invigorated, June closed the door to the staff room behind her and returned to her colleagues with a skip in her step and quietly singing a familiar tune.

"Once I was afraid I was petrified..."

Rita Kemp was the first to ask about Denis on June's return.

"He seems fine. He was watching telly and seemed settled enough," she lied. "Let's leave him for a little while and see what happens. Probably some twenty four hour bug he's got."

"Well I hope the randy old bugger's been given something to dampen his libido. Has he been married? Bet he never gave his missus a rest if he was. He must have been at it for hours to make his dangly bits so sore. It looked like a wizened plum tomato," Freda chipped in.

"I don't know anything about him. Is he a local chap?" June said, smirking at Freda's sarcastic comment.

"I'm sure I heard Sarah say he had moved back into the area a couple of years ago. You'd think he would have some family in the area. Maybe he never married," Freda casually replied.

Sarah Stead, being one of the three qualified nursing staff would have had access to all his notes so June had her question answered. She wondered what had made him return to Burtley after so many years.

The night had passed quite peacefully until 3.12am when an alarm bell could be heard down the first corridor. Again, June and the other two women were the first to see the light flashing on the board indicating the room number that had a resident in need of urgent assistance. Again it was room number five. Denis was in need of help once more.

Rita and Freda were quick off the mark and again never noticed June's hesitation as the two shot off down the corridor. She watched them disappear into Denis's room and felt a sudden strong griping pain spread across her abdomen. Fear and anticipation of what she may have caused had her scuttling to the staff toilet.

June had managed to slip out of the toilet without being seen. As she swiftly made her way back towards the central area and staff work station she looked up the corridor towards Denis's room and caught sight of Jean Hartley, the night shift's nurse opening the door to room number five. Something had happened to Denis that needed urgent medical attention. Had he had another stroke? She hoped not as she had not finished dishing out some rough justice to her abuser. He had to live a while longer.

It was about fifteen minutes before Jean, the nurse, came out of Denis's room. As she made her way back into the central area June could not stop herself from asking how he was.

"He's vomited all over the bed and followed through. What a mess. His temperature seems fine and his blood pressure's okay. It looks as if he has caught a virus. The girls are cleaning up and washing him down. You can take some clean bedding to them if you will, please. If you can find an air freshener it might help .It smells pretty bad in there."

"Right! I'll get some sheets sorted and there may be an aerosol in the loo." June knew that to be true as she had sprayed the toilet liberally after her urgent call of nature.

Clutching the clean bed linen and a can of air freshener to her chest June warily entered room number five. The stench of excrement and fresh vomit had instantly caused her to want to wretch. She instinctively sprayed the aerosol liberally in all directions in a desperate attempt to replace the sickening smell with a refreshing scent of lavender.

"It's a bit ripe in here. It's enough to make your eyes water," Freda said with a nasal tone to her voice. She was obviously trying not to breathe through her nose. June had already started to breathe through her mouth to block the smell and avoid gagging.

In the armchair beside his bed, Denis's face was a strange shade of grey. His frail body clothed in clean pyjamas had slumped to one side of the chair. He could easily have been mistaken for a corpse that had died in the chair.

When Freda and Rita had finally finished cleaning up the mess both were looking pale.

"What a bloody mess that was and the smell, well it'll take ages to clear the pong from my nostrils," Rita was the first comment.

"He looks dreadful. I reckon he needs to be seen by his doctor in the morning. That's if he makes it through the night of course," was Freda's concerned response.

June heard the comments made by both women and felt a wave of emotions sweep over her. She feared he may die and a post mortem would detect traces of salt and the syrup of figs in the contents of his stomach. But knowing that she had caused him so much upset was giving her a sense of satisfaction. She needed him to live a little longer simply because she had to make him suffer even more. A new plan of action would have to be made. She had plenty of ideas in mind to make the old man wish he had never come back to Burtley.

Her small stint on the night shift was completed and the first thing June wanted to do was have a hot shower and scrub away the gut churning odour that seemed to be clinging to her after being in Denis's room.

She'd felt pangs of guilt stabbing at her subconscious mind but the feelings were not of remorse for her actions. Her two colleagues had borne the brunt of the disgusting mess June had caused and she had no grudge to bear against them. She had already made her decision not to use the syringes again on Denis, praying that he would survive and not meet his maker for a while.

Even after a shower and covering her skin with perfumed body lotion, June still could not put the smell of Denis's projectile vomiting out of her mind. Again her thoughts were with the two women who had the task of cleaning up the mess. She would make sure that in future nobody else would suffer in her plight to seek revenge. With that thought in mind she'd crawled into bed for some much needed rest.

Sleep had come quickly but not been restful. June had slipped in and out of dreams that had been a mixture of old nightmares intermingled with the previous night's incidents. By mid-afternoon she was up and about and logged onto the internet.

Once again she had scoured the Amazon website and placed an order for hypodermic needles and some mini long nosed pliers. The entire cost was only a few pounds but would be worth the money she thought.

Her goods would not arrive for a few days which would be fine.

She needed to let Denis recover from his ordeal before she started her next phase of intimidation or even mild torture.

With the rest of the weekend free to do as she pleased, June decided a good spring clean of her flat was needed and would take her mind off of the previous night's events. She'd set about the task full of enthusiasm and with a spring in her step as she started humming the familiar lines of Gloria Gaynor's famous song.

After a full afternoon of vigorous cleaning June was still convinced she could still smell the stench of Denis's excrement and vomit. Not even a liberal spraying of surface cleaners and furniture polish could eliminate the odour from her nostrils. She knew it was all in her mind and her thoughts kept returning to her poor friends Rita and Freda. Had they managed to put the unsavoury incident behind them? The unfortunate pair had been up to their elbows in "sick n shit" according to Rita.

Another pang of guilt briefly passed through June's thoughts. But it was only brief.

Chapter 20

June drew back the curtains on Monday morning, looked outside and was surprised to see the ground covered in a layer of frost. She hadn't noticed a drop in temperature outside because she had spent the entire weekend in her cosy flat and been totally pre occupied in plotting a few surprises for a certain old man.

Some of her thoughts that had passed through her mind during the previous couple of days had been quite bizarre. She had visualised different ways of killing him. Strangulation had been the first scenario. Peering into his eyes, bulging from their sockets whilst she tightened her grip around his scraggy neck would be too obvious.

Then she'd thought about beating his head into a pulp. A baseball bat would have been her choice of weapon. With each blow to his head she would ask him why he did it. Seeing him terrified before the first blow cracked into his skull would give her some sense of satisfaction. The mess afterwards would have to be cleaned up by an innocent party. This was between her and Denis, so that thought lost some appeal.

Suffocating him with a pillow was the less gory method of extermination but she would not be able to see his face as he strived to draw his last breath. Covering his head with a plastic bag was another option that she had thought better of.

She yearned for the opportunity to release decades of pent up anger and slowly torture him in the most excruciating ways until he died. She wanted it to be her face that was the last thing he saw as he went to hell. As much as she didn't want to be jailed for his demise, at times she had thought it would be worth paying the price. Hadn't he already inflicted a mental prison sentence upon her that was far more punishing?

She was feeling very perky and refreshed as she ate toast and gulped down coffee whilst applying her make up. It had been over two days since she had last seen Denis. She was hoping her prayers had been answered and he had managed to recover sufficiently from his ordeal to allow her the pleasure of seeing him afraid once more. If anything had happened to him over the weekend all would be revealed at the morning meeting.

As she had expected, Maureen was on her way to work at the usual time and the two friends met on their short walk to Field Hall. And as usual Maureen had felt the need to update her friend on the trials and tribulations of the Jones family. With more pressing issues on her mind June let her friend do all the talking and as they neared their destination she felt a tightening in her chest. *Please let him be alive,* she wished silently.

After hanging up coats and securing handbags and valuables in their lockers, the two women made their way to the morning meeting. Palpitations had already started to trouble June. Her anxiety was sky high and she hoped no one would notice.

A sharp pain pierced her abdomen and the sudden urge to pass wind had her clenching her buttocks. She could not afford to dash off to the toilet and miss the morning's update.

The second that the morning's debriefing had finished June dashed to the staff toilets and allowed the muscles of her buttocks to relax. Within seconds her pain had eased as the trapped wind was released followed by an urgent bowel movement. She sighed with relief. Denis had survived.

Before leaving the toilet cubicle she put her hand in the pocket of her tunic and pulled out the specimen pot she had taunted him with a few nights earlier. It was time to have a little bit of fun with it again.

Back amongst the rest of the care team, June felt it would be only natural to enquire how Denis had been over the weekend. She asked Shirley Lee, one of the women who had been working over the weekend.

"Oh, he was really ill all day Saturday. A doctor came out to see him and prescribed something to stop the diarrhoea but he's in pads now as a precaution. I think he took a stool sample to be analysed for food poisoning or something. It was a bit of a mess I was told. He's picked up a bit, though he's only taking liquids and seems to want to stay in his room."

"I know. I saw the mess he was in. Well, as long as he's getting better now. I'll pop in and see him later. I was half expecting to be told he'd gone over the weekend," June replied in a fake concerned manner. "It would have been such a shame as he's only just getting settled in and getting to know us all. Let's hope he's with us a while longer."

As an afterthought she added "Does he have any close family who might want to visit?"

Shirley was quick to reply. "It appears he was born in Burtley but has been living down south for years and lost contact with them. It's a shame. He looks so vulnerable."

June had to bite her bottom lip. What she really wanted to do was shout, "fucking vulnerable, do me a fucking favour." Her use of vulgar expletives was becoming a common occurrence.

In the dining room most of the residents were having breakfast and sat alone at the far end of the room was the other new resident Ellen Gregson. Feeling a little sorry for her, June decided she would go cheer her up.

"Good morning Ellen. How are you settling in? Do you like your room? They are nice and cosy. Your in room nine aren't you?"

She nodded and gave her a weak smile exposing a set of upper dentures that made June immediately think of Red Rum the race horse.

"You'll soon make friends and this will start to feel like it's your home. Eat up. You've got to keep your strength up." She patted the back of the old ladies small wrinkled hand, turned and walked away.

Shirley was just entering the dining room and as the pair passed each other June asked "Is anyone with Denis? I'll go say hello and see how he is."

"Don't think anyone is with him and the buzzer hasn't gone off. Go and see the poor old soul."

"Will do. If I'm wanted you know where I am."

Clutching the little pot in her pocket June headed off towards room number five.

Turning her head in all directions to make sure there were no other residents or staff lurking along the corridor, June gently knocked on the door of number five and opened it just a little. Peering round the corner of the door she looked straight at the old man propped up in his bed.

"Morning Denis. How are you feeling today?"

His pale, almost skull like head turned towards the door. On seeing June`s face he quickly looked away.

Closing the door behind her, she walked up to the bed and clasped her left hand over his jaw and forced him to turn his head and look at her. He closed his eyes as small tears formed in the corners.

"Closing your eyes won`t make me go away Denis so look at me."

His eyes remained closed and tears began to roll down his cheeks.

"I said fucking look at me you piece of shit!"

His eyes still remained closed.

"Please your fucking self. I`ve brought a little friend to see you. You remember him don`t you? He`s got a lot of hairy legs to crawl over you with. Shall I let him loose in the bed then?"

His eyes opened wide. She saw fear in his teary eyes and smiled.

"Frightened are we Denis? Well here he is." She pulled the little pot out of her pocket and shook it.

"Incey Wincey spider climbing up the spout. I`m going to let old Incey Wincey out," she sang in a low voice.

Releasing his jaw, June unscrewed the lid of the pot then grabbed his jaw again forcing his mouth open.

"Here he comes Denis," she said as the contents of the pot dropped into his mouth.

She kept a firm grip on his jaw as the old man stuck out his tongue and started shaking his head to dislodge the spider. His body jerked as he made throaty moaning sounds and his face started to turn a ruddy shade as he fought against the strong grip of June`s hand. He was overcome by panic.

Releasing her grip on him, she snatched up the spider that had been placed on his tongue and held it up for him to see. Moving her face as close as possible she whispered, "Had you going there Denis. Bet you've crapped yourself again. You dirty, despicable piece of shit. Remembered who I am yet? We'll have some more fun later. You'll like that won't you?"

Stepping back from the bed, June turned and walked over to the door. As she was leaving the room she turned around and held out her hand. On her palm lay the green spiky stalk of a tomato.

Closing the door quietly behind her she set off back down the corridor with a beaming smile that not even a Cheshire cat could compete with.

June had not long been back in the dining room when she heard the unmistakable sound of an alarm ringing. Her heart missed a beat as she saw a couple of the other members of staff scurrying towards the central area and then head off down the corridor she had just returned from. Her mouth became so dry she could barely swallow. She just knew it was Denis who had raised the alarm.

Chapter 21

The events of the previous day had been playing on June's mind so badly that she had only managed a couple of hours of sleep when the alarm clock started ringing in her ears. Bleary eyed and drowsy, she reached out, fumbled for the snooze button and heaved a big sigh.

Her first waking thought had been about Denis and the panic attack that she had caused him to have. Tormenting him with the tomato stalk had given her a lot of pleasure and it had certainly had the desired effect she had wanted. He'd lost control of his bowels and bladder as she suspected he would but the mess had been contained in the incontinence pad he had been wearing.

The two women who had responded to his alarm had been over half an hour before they left his room. June had overheard them telling the shift's nurse that he had been very distressed and had been trying to tell them something. Unfortunately, he had not been able to make them understand what had caused him to freak out, which was what June had been relying on.

When she had arrived home on Monday evening, waiting in her mail box in the entrance foyer was her parcel from Amazon. She was ready to start the next phase of torment on a frightened old man.

Up, showered and dressed, June fancied a cooked breakfast. She put bacon under the grill and while waiting for it to cook she fetched her new purchases from the lounge and placed them on the kitchen worktop.

The small pliers just needed to be laid flat in the bottom of her tunic pocket but a hypodermic needle needed some additions to it before it could go in.

The night before, June had rifled to the back of a kitchen drawer and found a champagne cork that had been lurking there for ages. She'd forgotten why it had been kept and doubted it had ever been in a real champagne bottle. A bottle of cheap sparkling wine had probably been its place of origin.

Pushing one end of the needle into the cork would stop June from piercing her hand when she held it and a small piece of Blue Tack on the other end would make sure it did not protrude through the fabric of her tunic. With the needle safe to handle, June placed it carefully into her pocket. She was ready for action and ready to tuck into her morning fry up.

It was almost lunchtime before June found an opportunity to pay a visit to Denis. Still refusing to leave his room a couple of the staff members had made sure he had eaten some breakfast and given him a bath. June knew she would have to take a chance on not being seen when she idled up the corridor towards his room, hoping no one would notice she had gone missing.

Instead of slowly entering room number five as in previous visits, June made a quick scan of her surroundings and slyly made her entrance. She had caught Denis totally by surprise. His face said more than any words ever could.

On seeing her face he recoiled against the propped pillows on his bed. The colour drained from his tired facial features.

"Hello Denis. Been waiting for me have you? Shall we have some more fun?" June said with a laugh.

There was no response to her questions.

She reached into her tunic pocket and grabbed the hypodermic needle, pulled off the small piece of Blue Tack and held it up for Denis to see. His face showed no flicker of emotion.

June walked directly towards the bed and sat on the edge, trapping Denis's left arm beneath her. She had him totally immobilised.

"You don't like needles Denis do you? How do I know that? Have you remembered who I am yet? I know everything about you."

Still he showed no emotion even as she held the needle dangerously close to his left eye.

"You never did like needles, did you? Wouldn't go to the dentist either would you? I can see you have a few rotten teeth Denis. Perhaps I should pull them out for you just to spare you the pain of toothache of course." She grabbed his jaw and yanked his mouth wide open. "Open wide Denis," she ordered.

His facial expression still didn`t alter. Small teardrops trickled over his sunken cheekbones as June jabbed the needle into his upper gum, just enough to break the skin. Quickly the needle was returned to her pocket and replaced by the small pliers held firmly in her hand.

"I`ll go easy on you today Denis. Just the one tooth needs attention," she said, then gripped a broken tooth on the upper left side of his mouth with the pliers.

"I`m not going to pull it today Denis. I`ll just loosen it a bit." As she spoke she forced the plier upwards forcing the tooth to retract slightly into his gum. He moaned and she felt his body go tense.

Keeping a firm grip of the broken molar she wiggled it from side to side, just enough to feel it loosen. In an instant the pliers were back inside her pocket and she had released her grip on his jaw.

June looked directly into her victim`s eyes clouded with tears, now streaming down his face and wetting the collar of his pyjamas.

"I`m going now Denis. Remember now, this is just our little secret. Just a bit of fun we`re having together. Can you remember the fun we used to have when I was a little girl? I do!"

Before he had time to make any response June was out of his room and sauntering back down the corridor.

In room number five Denis Goodman lay holding his left hand up to his cheek. A dull throbbing ache had started in his upper gum.

How did she know he hated needles and spiders? Who was she?

Two thoughts were foremost in his mind but another more daunting thought quickly replaced them. *What was she going to do to him next time?*

Chapter 22

Wednesday morning had started out in the normal way for June. She had slept much better than the previous night and made herself another full English breakfast. A couple of flashbacks of her visit into Denis's room had interrupted her television viewing the night before but not caused her to worry too much. For the rest of her shift there had been no resident's alarm bells ringing after her attempts at amateur dentistry. She assumed he had kept quiet about it. Now he knew what it was like to be afraid and not dare tell anyone.

June would have to be vigilante again and try to find some more time to be alone with her uncle. Needle and pliers were again safely tucked into her tunic pocket ready for action when an opportunity presented itself.

The morning changeover meeting had been just routine information apart from staff being asked to pay particular attention to one chap who's dementia seemed to be getting worse. He had been in a very agitated mood through the night and spent most of it wandering in and out of his room and disturbing some of the other residents. A visit from his doctor had been requested for that day.

There was no mention of Denis Goodman which was more of a relief than June had expected it to be. She had been sailing a little too close to the wind, as her late mother would have said.

Having to spend far more time than usual attending to the dementia sufferer's nocturnal wanderings had put extra pressure on the night shift workers. Some of the residents who were early risers had been waiting longer than usual for help to get up, washed and dressed for breakfast. The women set about getting everyone sorted and set up for the day.

June made a point of avoiding being the one who assisted Denis. She didn't want anyone suspecting she was spending time alone with him. It was her friend Maureen who took care of him that morning. June went into Ellen Gregson's room and helped her bathe and dress.

It was almost time to serve lunch before June felt she may be able to sneak into room number five. There had been no sign of Denis in the dining room at breakfast or in the sitting room. The only assumption she could make was that he had stayed in his room again. She dare not ask about him but was keeping a wary eye on the comings and goings of everyone.

After lunch, convinced the coast was clear, June ambled up the corridor trying to act as natural as possible. If any beady eyed member of staff did spot her she had decided her excuse would be that she had left her watch in Ellen's room which was directly across from Denis's.

She didn't knock on the door, just opened it and slipped inside. Denis was still sat propped up in his bed. His face turned a sickly shade of grey as he caught sight of June staring directly at him with a leering smile on her face.

"Hello Denis. Are you sure you don't know who I am? Look at my badge Denis. What does it say? It says my name is June. Ring any bells yet? Maybe a little bit of pain will help you remember."

He didn't flinch when she spoke to him or as she went over to his bedside and sat on his arm to pin him to the bed.

"I won't use the needle today. I haven't got much time. Just a little bit more treatment on your teeth," she said as her left hand once again forced him to open his mouth wide.

Her other hand fumbled for the pliers in her pocket. Just as she pulled them out the door opened behind her. June turned her head around to see who was behind her. Maureen was stood by the door looking confused.

"What the hell are you doing?"

June's mouth had gone so dry she could not answer.

"June, what's going on? Get off of him! Can't you see you're hurting him?"

She stood up and walked towards Maureen but still couldn't get any words out.

"June, for God's sake what's matter with you? Have you gone bonkers? What do you want these things for?" she asked as she grabbed the pliers from June's hand.

June gulped and managed to make enough saliva to say, "I can explain."

"You can explain. Explain what exactly? I saw you sitting on him and what you were about to do to his face, I wouldn't like to hazard a guess."

"I can explain but not here. It's not what you think it is. Well, yes you did see me sat on him but it's ..."

"It's what exactly? You've put me in a dreadful position June. I thought I knew you but ...."

"You do know me Maureen and you know I would never hurt anyone. Please let me explain."

"You know I have to report what I've just seen. Jesus Christ June, I can't pretend I never saw you."

"I know, I know, I know," June replied pathetically and continued to plead, "Please, because of our friendship give me a chance to explain. When you've heard it all then I won't stop you from reporting me. In fact, I'll go and tell Mrs. McClellan what I've done."

"Right, go ahead and explain. I'm all ears," Maureen answered impatiently.

"Not here. I need to explain everything and not just what you've just seen. Can you come to mine after work? I promise you tomorrow we'll go to McClellan's office together," June begged her friend.

"I'll give you five minutes but can't see what difference it's going to make. Just keep your distance from me for the rest of the day. Now get out and I'll see to Denis. He looks petrified. Poor sod."

June left her friend fussing over the old man. As she walked back down the corridor she could be heard muttering "Shit, shit, shit."

93

Chapter 23

As the two women walked out of Field Hall that evening, the atmosphere between them could have been cut with a knife. Neither spoke or even looked at each other. The short walk to June`s flat was usually a time when the two friends chewed over the day`s events, but not that day.

June punched in the security number to her flat and held open the outer communal door to allow Maureen to pass into the hall. They walked the few steps to the inner door still maintaining the uncomfortable silence. Even as June unlocked the door to her flat and stood aside to let her friend enter first, Maureen still avoided eye contact and didn`t offer a polite, "thank you".

She wouldn`t even remove her shoes or take off her coat as she had always done when visiting her friend. Maureen was making it obvious that five minutes was all she was going to spare to listen to June`s excuse for what she considered despicable behaviour.

"Please, sit down Maureen," June pleaded with her friend. "Please."

With a huge, impatient sigh she walked over to the large leather armchair and perched her behind on the edge of the seat. Her body language spoke volumes.

June in turn sat on her sofa and for the second time that day her mouth was so dry she could barely swallow. Her hands had started to shake and clasping her fingers together didn`t stop their tremor.

"God, I need a drink," June managed to say as she got up and made her way over to the sideboard and slid open the door.

Her medicinal bottle of brandy still had a small amount in it and in one quick manoeuvre she had unscrewed the top and gulped down a mouthful straight from the bottle.

"Bloody hell, you`ve really lost the plot," a bewildered Maureen quipped.

It took only a couple of seconds for the brandy to do its job. As the warm liquid slid down the back of her throat the knot in her stomach seemed to loosen. June took a deep breath and started to speak.

"You know that I was an only child and I told you how my mum was when it came to being prim n proper about everything. Well..."

Before June could say anymore, Maureen interrupted her with, "What the hell has your chuffing mother got to do with anything?"

"Please! Just bloody listen and don`t interrupt me. I have to tell you it all to make any sense of it. Please just let me explain!"

Maureen blew out a sigh but nodded her head.

"I`ve told you I don`t have many relatives still alive only a cousin and her kids who I never see."

Maureen nodded again.

"Well, I have an uncle, my mother`s brother. I`ve never spoken about him. He disappeared to London or somewhere down south years ago and I assumed he was dead. I hoped he was dead."

A small tear ran down her face as she spoke.

"Well, he`s not dead and he`s not down south anymore. He`s here in Burtley."

Maureen looked across at June who was about to sit down on the sofa. For the first time since they had entered the flat, she looked her in the eye and saw a trickle of tears that were dripping from her friend`s chin and wetting her tunic.

"I don`t understand," she said in a much gentler manner.

"My long lost uncle is Denis Goodman."

"What? You never said when he arrived. So, what was today all about then?" Maureen was confused and it showed in her expression.

"I`m going to tell you why and you will be the only person I have ever told apart from a therapist. Even then I never told her the whole story."

Now she had her friend`s undivided attention.

June started to recount her early childhood memories and how close she had been to her uncle. When she got to the stage where she had started to have piano lessons, she could feel her throat start to tighten but forced herself to continue. Reaching the part where Denis had started his abuse, her emotions overtook her. She couldn't contain them any longer and tears started to run like rivulets over her now blotchy red cheeks.

"Jesus Christ!" was the only expression Maureen could get out as a tear started to roll down her own face.

She stood up and walked over to her friend, sat beside her on the sofa and reached out her hand for June to grasp. With their free hands both women wiped away their own tears. Neither could speak.

A few minutes passed in total silence apart from an occasional sob that June could not supress. The silence was not awkward anymore.

June felt comforted by her friend's squeezing of her hand which she grasped tightly as she struggled to gain control of her tears. She knew it was time to tell someone all the sordid details and was glad it was Maureen who she was going to unburden her soul to.

"What happened after he started touching you? Did you tell your parents?" Maureen was the first to break the silence.

"No. It didn't stop there." June carried on recounting her sickening story. She avoided eye contact with her friend as she spoke. Her familiar feelings of shame were present and obvious.

"He forced you to give him a blow job! The fucking evil bastard!" Maureen was never one to use foul language but it seemed she was prepared to make an exception on this occasion.

"What did he say after he'd done all this to you? Did he say he was sorry? What?"

"He just carried on as normal as if what he'd done was okay but he always insisted it was our little secret. How could I tell my mother what he'd done? She was so close to her little brother I doubt she would have believed a word of it. I was so ashamed and it always felt like it was my fault. I never tried to run away, I was so frightened I just froze when he touched me," June answered apologetically.

"Don't make bloody excuses for the bastard. He was the adult. No, not an adult, he was...he was a bloody disgusting pervert."

"That's not everything he made me do."

"Jesus, what else is there he could do? Except..." Maureen turned and looked at her friend as she said the dreaded word, "rape...he didn't! Please say he didn't go that far."

June's face had the answer written all over it.

"He did didn't he? He fucking did."

Several minutes passed before June regained her composure and continued telling her friend all the seedy details of Denis Goodman's perverted antics. With each revelation she included the most intimate of details and though she felt ashamed at allowing the abuse to happen, slowly the burden she had been carrying round for four decades seemed to feel much lighter.

Maureen had stayed silent as the details of the rape were recounted in minute detail. Her only response was the shaking of her head and a grimaced expression on her face. It was obvious June felt the need to go over every little detail. Her tears had dried up and her apologetic attitude was slowly turning into anger.

It had been over an hour since the two women had arrived at June's flat and though Maureen had initially agreed to stay only five minutes she was showing no signs of wanting to leave. As June finally came to the end of her sad, sorry saga she gave a big sigh and said, "So now you know it all."

"Well I could do with a cup of tea after hearing all that. Stick the kettle on," Maureen said trying to lighten the atmosphere.

"Don't you have to get off home?"

"Nah, they'll all be out anyway so I'll be sat on my own all night. Anyway, there's still something you haven't told me."

"What?"

"Errrr, the pliers. Where do they feature in all this?"

"I'll put the kettle on then."

Chapter 24

For the first time in forty long, lonely years June Cowburn felt free. Free at last from the clutches of her rapist. She had finally confided in someone and was so pleased that the certain someone was her friend Maureen. Now, with nothing to hide she could tell her friend everything. She was alone no more.

"So, your mum and dad never suspected a thing. Are you sure it wasn`t a case of not wanting to know the truth? You`ve said she hated tittle tattle and refused to gossip with the neighbours. Well what if she did suspect something was wrong but couldn`t face being the butt of her neighbours chit chat. Let`s face it, it would have been bad enough having to handle you being abused but when the pervert was her own brother...well! What a field day the neighbours would have had if that had all come out in the wash."

June took a sip of her tea before responding to the allegations about her parents.

"I don`t think my dad had any idea. No, I`m sure he didn`t. The problem was that Denis just behaved as he normally would whenever we were all together. He`d still try to kiss me like a loving uncle and there was never anything that he said or did that would have warning bells ringing. No, my mum probably just thought I was being a stroppy teenager when I started spending more time in my room. I loved going to see my grandparents and he made it so I couldn`t face the car journeys to visit them. They thought I didn`t want to see them anymore. He made me hurt everyone I cared about just so I could avoid being with him. Hate doesn`t come near what I feel for that man."

"Hang on a minute. Did you say earlier that I`m the only person who knows?" Maureen knew that what she had just said was true, but was leading their conversation in another direction. "Because if I am then it means you didn`t tell your husband. Why not?"

"Hindsight is a wonderful thing. Nigel was a lovely man and I wanted to make him happy but the stumbling block was Denis. It always came down to him. I made Nigel wait until we were married before we had sex and he accepted it. He knew about my mum and her views about being permissive so he assumed I was the same. He never really tried to change my mind. But it was nothing to do with my mother. I froze whenever he got too close."

It was time to fill her friend in on the real reason her marriage had ended and take the blame away from Nigel.

"I could never get rid of the feeling that I was doing something disgusting. He wanted to please me and I just lay there gritting my teeth just wanting it to be over as quickly as possible. Sometimes, Nigel would make a noise when he was...you can imagine...and it would remind me of the noises Denis Goodman made when he had me pinned down. You've heard of lie back and think of England, well I couldn't even do that. I just wanted to be left alone...for Denis to leave me alone. How do you explain that to your husband?"

"Right, so Nigel looked elsewhere for sex. Understandable I suppose. To his credit he did put up with it for years before he left," Maureen added.

"I don't blame Nigel for anything. He was a decent bloke and I actually loved him in the only way I could. But that's not good enough for any man. So, Denis took away more than my virginity. He took away my one real chance of finding happiness. And, he may not have been physically responsible but I can't help blaming him for my miscarriage."

"A miscarriage! You've never mentioned that before."

"Nobody ever asked. It was early on in our marriage and before you ask, I was as surprised as you are now when I realised I was pregnant."

June was on a roll now and she didn't seem to be able to stop. Words just kept on coming.

"November 19th 1996 was the day all chances of Nigel and me being happy together were quashed. We were actually looking forward to having a baby and I think we could have had a reasonably happy life together as a family. It may have made up for the poor sex life we had. But a baby never materialised. The next few years we spent just living under the same roof really."

"I can't believe you've managed to cover all this up from everyone. You never ever gave us a hint of what you've experienced. You're usually the one who cheers us up and makes everybody laugh."

"I've been living the past few years behind a painted smile," was June's sad explanation.

Maureen could see that June was getting teary eyed again so changed the subject by reverting to the previous revelations.

"So, when did you find out Denis was back in Burtley?"

"The day he arrived at Field Hall. I saw his face as they wheeled him in but couldn't be certain until I was told his name. Have you noticed the blemish on his cheek? It's faded slightly and his eyes have lost of the intensity they had when he used to glare at me while he was ... God knows where he's been hiding for the past forty years and why has he come back here? He's back to spoil my life all over again."

"He's not going to spoil anything ever again for you," Maureen was offering her reassurance.

"It's a bit late to say that. I've as good as dismissed myself from a job I love. McClellan will have me banished from the building the second she hears what I've done," June responded with a shrug of her shoulders. "I'll probably end up in court if not in prison."

Maureen sipped the last drop of tea from her cup and stood up.

"If I sit here any longer I'll take root and I'm getting hungry. Forget McClellan. It's almost nine o clock. I need to go but I'll come back tomorrow after work and you can fill me in on the rest then. It's been a lot to digest tonight. My head's spinning and you look worn out."

The two women got up from the sofa and walked to the hallway.

Maureen picked up her coat and shoes on the way. She had eventually removed them once her mood had changed.

June opened the door and was taken by complete surprise as her friend wrapped her arms around her and planted a kiss on her forehead. They had never exchanged hugs and kisses before.

"You're not on your own now June. I'll see you tomorrow. It's going to be just another day at the office. Get some rest."

June closed the door and leaned back against it. She gave out yet another large sigh as tears started to well up in her eyes again. This time they were tears of joy and relief.

Chapter 25

Thursday passed without any problems. The two friends had walked to work together as they always did but neither mentioned what had been discussed the night before. The awkward atmosphere that had been prevalent the day before, that had been almost unbearable for both women, had disappeared and been replaced by a new closeness. They now shared one massive secret.

No reports had been made about Denis and his physical state but he was still being reluctant to come out of his room. June had got away with her antics yet again.

As promised, Maureen walked home with her friend and this time made herself immediately at home.

"Stick the kettle on and I could manage a biscuit if you`ve got one, chuck." She only ever used the word chuck when she was in a good or mischievous mood.

June did as asked and the two women were soon huddled together on the sofa, complete with a mug of tea and a Kit Kat each. Neither was sure who should bring up the sensitive topic of conversation but it was Maureen who plunged in first.

"Last night I couldn`t get my head round a lot of what you told me. I was so gobsmacked at all the stuff he had...forced you to do, I didn`t take much notice of some things you said. Anyway, I was trying to read my book in bed last night and still thinking about it when I had a "Eureka!" moment. I`ve thought of nothing else all day and I think I`ve sussed something you might be interested to hear."

June was just about to take a bite of her biscuit but stopped dead.

"I`m all ears."

"When he started touching you ... and such, did you say it was while you were having piano lessons at his house?

"Mmm."

"I told you when I was a kid our grandma lived with us. Well, she played the piano. Usually she only played at family do's and such. More of a Mrs. Mill's type pub pianist. Anyway..." Maureen stopped to take a deep breath before continuing, "When our gran died we were left with her old piano and none of us could play it, except for our Kathleen, who had picked up a few tunes that she could knock out on the black keys. So, our mum was all set to try and sell it and went to put an advert in the newsagents. Well, she never put the ad in because she got chatting to the woman in the shop and she suggested letting one of us three having lessons. Better still, there was an advert in the shop window advertising piano lessons. I wasn't interested, nor our Graham, but our Kathleen quite fancied having a go." Maureen gulped down a big swig from her mug of tea before she continued.

"From what I can remember because I would only be about nine or ten at the time, our Kathleen had a few lessons. Now this is where it gets interesting." Another drink and she continued, "One tea time our Kathleen came back from her piano lesson and I can remember our mum pushing me and our Graham out of the kitchen and closing the door. When we tried to go back in we were pushed back out and our mum said she needed to talk to our Kathleen alone. I tried listening with my ear to the door and all I could catch was our mum saying that our dad would go mad when he found out."

June stayed silent and was hanging on to every word her friend was saying.

"I'm almost certain that it was the same night that my parents had a big argument. I remember our dad coming home from work and after we'd had tea our mum pushed us three out of the kitchen and closed the door. It went quiet but I could hear our mum's voice talking to dad and then he started shouting. Our dad stormed out of the kitchen and went upstairs with our mum running after him. I'm sure she kept telling him not to do anything stupid."

Another swig of her tea and she was ready to continue telling her tale.

"I'm almost certain that our dad went out that night and left our mum crying upstairs. She came down and her eyes were red. When

103

our dad came back later he was in a right mood. They closed the kitchen door again and I heard our mum shouting. The one thing I can remember hearing is her saying the police might come. They never did as far as I know but why would she think the police might come?"

"Are we thinking the same thing here?" June replied inquisitively.

"All I know is our Kathleen never had another piano lesson after that night. What do you make of that?"

June stayed silent.

"What if it was Denis who was the piano teacher and...maybe he had done something he shouldn`t to our Kathleen? That would be a good enough reason for our dad to blow his top. I think he went round there and smacked him one," Maureen concluded.

"Where did this chap live?"

"Lower Burtley Road" both women said in unison.

After a couple of minutes with both women sat deep in thought June broke the silence.

"When did all this happen?"

"Err, our gran died the day before Halloween 1971 so it would be early in the new year because we still had the piano at Christmas."

"And Denis cleared off in February 1972. That`s a bit too much of a coincidence," June concluded.

"I`d say so. Do you reckon he did a runner because our dad had a go at him? He might have been afraid he was going to be reported to the police," Maureen surmised.

"It would explain an awful lot. Christ it would have killed my mother if she`d have ever found out about him," June said with a hint of sadness in her voice.

The two friends sat in complete silence contemplating what they had discussed. In the past forty eight hours, between them they had opened a can of worms and there was no way those worms would go back into the can. The women had been good friends but were now sharing a bond neither could ever have imagined.

Chapter 26

It was almost lunchtime when June finally dragged her body out of bed that day. She had managed almost twelve hours of undisturbed sleep. For the first time in weeks she'd managed to let her head hit the pillow and drift away without reliving the events of the day. Being Friday and with three rest days in front of her she had time to plan her next little surprise.

With all the revelations and conclusions the friends had shared, it occurred to June that she had still not explained to Maureen what she had been up to with the pliers. Denis's past life and antics had become their prior concern.

After a couple of hours of catching up on housework and a huge pile of dirty washing, June made herself a caffeine fix and flopped down on her sofa. An air of calmness had replaced the knot in her stomach she had been carrying around for the past few days. Just as she was getting comfy with her feet up on the sofa her mobile phone started to blast out Dolly Parton's "Nine to five".

"June, it's me. I'm coming round so get the kettle on." Maureen sounded excited.

Within ten minutes the friends were drinking coffee and dunking Hob Nobs. Maureen had made herself comfy on the sofa and started to reveal the reason for her impromptu visit.

"I've been on the phone to our Kathleen this morning and before you start, I didn't tell her anything about you. I made up a story about somebody I know who got talking about piano lessons as a kid. She's no reason to think I'm telling her a porky. I had my fingers crossed anyway. So, I asked her why she gave up lessons so suddenly. I made out this woman had said something about the teacher touching her and so she stopped going for lessons and that he was a local chap. She swallowed it and when I asked her if that was why she gave up she said …yes."

"Do you swear that you never mentioned me?"

"I swear. I asked her if what I remembered about our dad being mad was true. I was right. He did go round to see the piano teacher and sorted him out. It was our dad who stopped our Kathleen going again and he must have told her, that he had told the teacher he was going to report him to the police. From what our Kathleen says, Denis only started stroking her face and neck and she didn`t like it, so she told our mum. It all kicked off from there."

June took a sip of her coffee and dunked another biscuit before commenting.

"So, he did a runner after all. What I want to know now is what has he been doing since then and why has he come back here?"

"Well, I`ve thought about that as well and I may be able find out."

"How?"

"What does our Gary do for a living? He`s a copper and if anyone can find out where he`s been hiding then he can." Gary was Maureen`s second son and she was very proud of him and how well he was progressing in the police force.

"I`m going to see if he can do a bit of detective work and see just what Denis Goodman has been up to."

The pair sat in silence for a few more minutes, drinking their coffee and pondering over the new information that Maureen`s sister had revealed.

"Is now a good time to tell you what I was doing with the pliers?" June felt it was only right to confess to her friend about the torment she had recently inflicted on a defenceless old man.

"As good as any I suppose. After all what you`ve told me I doubt I`ll be shocked."

"I know he`s an old man now and very frail but just looking at him makes me want to hurt him so badly and kill him even. I still see the man who enjoyed forcing me to do disgusting things with him. He had me living in fear of ever being alone with him. I want him to feel the same things. I want my face to be the last thing he sees when he dies. So, I`ve been sneaking into his room and doing a few things to him."

"Such as?" Maureen asked wryly.

"Well you know when he was ill a few days ago, it was me who caused it all. I volunteered to do night duty so I had a better chance of getting him alone. Anyway, so far I've used itching powder on his genitals and that made him scratch until he was red raw. I forced syrup of figs and salt water down his throat and it made him chuck up and crap himself. I did feel guilty about that though. Poor Freda and Shirley copped for cleaning up the mess he made. Then, I remembered his phobia about spiders."

"Spiders?" She had her friend's undivided attention now.

June went on to explain her actions with the spider and the tomato stalk which brought a smile to her friend's face. Then she went on to explain her attempts at amateur dentistry.

"My God! I'm surprised he's still here after all that." Her friend was truly shocked at what she had just heard.

"Remind me never to make an enemy of you."

"Don't worry, you're safe. But I'm not going to rest until I've had my pound of flesh. I can't forget what he's done and just carry on as normal. I want him to beg for forgiveness even if he can only manage to make a pathetic groan. And then I want to see him well and truly dead." June's voice was full of determination and hatred.

"Look June, I can fully understand how you must feel but I don't want to be a part of whatever you have planned for him. But, I won't report you and I'm not going to try and stop you. I will try and watch your back though and will be praying you don't get caught."

"Fair enough. It's just between me and him. I wouldn't expect you or anyone else to put their job on the line. He's done enough damage without spoiling anyone else's life."

"I could manage another coffee and biscuit if there's one going begging, chuck." Maureen was in a mischievous mood.

Chapter 27

After another good night's sleep June decided she was going to spend all day Saturday pampering herself. Her eyebrows were in need of a good plucking and her skin would benefit from a good cleansing and moisturising. She had been so consumed in her vindictive capers that even her fingernails had been left to snag and peel. A decent manicure was in order and she had a nice new bottle of nail polish that had not been opened.

Maureen had suggested the two friends had a night out together and a mutual decision was made to treat themselves to a nice meal out, followed by a visit to the cinema.

As punctual as ever, Maureen arrived at her friend's flat dead on 7pm. She couldn't contain her excitement as she brushed past June in the hallway without taking off her shoes and headed for the lounge. She plonked herself down on the sofa and immediately started talking.

"Guess what?" She didn't wait for June to answer before she continued, "I know where Denis has been staying these past years."

June was checking the contents of her handbag while her friend was speaking but stopped what she was doing immediately on hearing her last comment. An uncomfortable tightness in her chest took her by surprise but she managed to ask the obvious question.

"Where?"

"Would you believe he's been in prison? Our Gary has been a little star and managed to find out what he's been up to. You were right about him moving down to the London area. He must have set himself up as a piano teacher and got up to his disgusting behaviour again. But, he was reported by one family and when the police made enquiries about his antics with some of his other pupils they confirmed everything. The poor kids had been too frightened to tell their parents about him."

June stood staring at her friend, in awe of what she had just heard.

"I think our Gary said he'd been released about three years ago. He must have been up to his antics for years before he was caught. I wonder how many poor kids are still having nightmares about the bastard. Well, they won't be kids anymore will they? The poor sods will be grown up now. It just doesn't bear thinking about."

As June tried to take in what her friend had been saying she felt like a deflating balloon. Her strength was sapped from her. She walked over to the sofa and flopped down beside Maureen.

"It wasn't my fault, it wasn't my fucking fault. All these years I've lived with the guilt for years thinking that I should have stopped him, could have stopped him. It wasn't me at all, it was that fucking creature's fault, not mine."

Tears filled June's eyes and mascara was starting to run down to her cheeks.

In another unusual display of affection, Maureen put her arms around her friend and pulled her close. For the first time in her life, June Cowburn let her guard down and allowed the warmth and compassion of her one true friend to surround her.

Maureen cradled June in her arms, holding her as if her life depended on it. As the tears streamed down her friend's face she whispered gently in her ear, "Let it all go. He can't hurt you anymore. Just let it all out."

It was almost ten minutes before June stopped sobbing on her friend's shoulder and throughout that time Maureen had constantly whispered reassuring words in her ear.

All plans that had been made to have a girlie night out had been washed away with the river of June's tears. Her friend had been unable to supress a few tears of her own and so both women finished up with blotchy faces and panda eyes. It was not the look that June had wished to achieve when she had spent the entire day preening herself.

A frozen pizza and a bag of chocolate raisins in front of the television seemed the perfect substitute for the cinema. There would be other nights out for the friends to enjoy.

Chapter 28

When the two women met up on their walk to work that Monday morning there appeared to be nothing different about the short journey, but there was one big difference. Thanks to Maureen`s detective work June was finally free from the curse of Denis Goodman. Added to that was the comfort of the close bond the two women had formed. She finally had a true friend and with that knowledge she felt even more determined to see that Denis should get some of his just desserts.

Before the weekend started June had wanted revenge for the misery he had caused her but now she was a woman on a mission. A mission to make a certain convicted paedophile regret he ever laid a single finger on every single one of the innocent children he had abused. She was going to make him wish he was dead and determined to send him on his way to hell.

After going through the routine of hanging up their coats and locking up there bags and valuables, June put her hand in the pocket of her tunic to feel the contents. The needle and pliers were tucked in the corner. This time she was calm and threw a knowing glance across to her friend, who in return gave a sly wink. It was game on.

At the morning meeting Denis`s name had been mentioned briefly. He had been spending most of his time in his room. It had been noted that he was not making any attempt to socialise and preferred to be alone. All staff members were asked to keep an eye on him. June was happy to do just that.

The night shift were again behind with getting everyone up and dressed due to the nocturnal antics of Wee Willie Winkie, the dementia sufferer, as he was now known to the staff. His condition was becoming more severe and causing disruption for the other residents. His time at Field Hall was coming to an end and a transfer to a specialist nursing home was on the cards.

Denis Goodman was one of those still waiting to be attended to. Before anyone else could speak, Maureen volunteered to sort him out.

The meeting was dissolved and the staff members all went about their business. Maureen sidled alongside her friend.

"Give me fifteen minutes with him then come and relieve me. I feel an urgent dash to the loo coming on," she whispered in her ear. The two exchanged a knowing look.

"Morning Denis, let's have you up and bathed. We're running a bit late this morning but I'll have you ready for your breakfast in no time," Maureen reassured him as she entered his room.

It took a few minutes to help him out of his bed and let him shuffle into the bathroom with minimal assistance. The bathroom was equipped with the luxury of a Bellavita bathlift, an aid designed to give as much independence as possible to the infirm.

The bathlift was controlled by a remote pad. Just a touch of a button raised the seat up or down; in our out of the water.

Maureen had managed to get Denis undressed and disposed of the sweaty, soiled incontinence pad he had been wearing while the bath was filling. Thanks to a few doses of syrup of figs secretly administered to him under duress, staff had thought it best if the pads became a permanent addition to his underwear. It was obvious to Maureen that the old man was not amused at being trussed up in adult nappies.

Getting him into the bath was easy with the bathlift and within a few minutes Denis was emerged up to his chest in the warm soapy water.

June sneaked into room number five as planned. On hearing her enter, Maureen called out to her friend, "June, can you keep an eye on Denis while I nip to the loo? I'm bursting."

"Of course I can. We're mates now aren't we Denis?" was her reply as she looked directly into the eyes of a worried old man. "Off you go. No need to rush back. I'll see to him."

She waited until Maureen had closed the door behind her then slowly walked over to the frail skeletal like body in the bath.

If looks could kill, Denis Goodman's life would have ended that very moment.

"I think we need to wash your hair Denis," she suggested reaching up for the shower head. Holding it in her right hand, with her free hand she grabbed a bottle of shampoo from the bath side and squeezed out a dollop onto the head of thinning grey hair. She allowed the bottle to drop onto the tiled floor as she briskly rubbed the lotion into Denis's scalp. Not once did he move. He was frozen with fear. *And so he should be*, she'd thought.

June grabbed a clump of his soapy hair and pulled his head backwards while using her other hand to turn the lever on the tap to cold. One pull and the lever moved to the shower position. A jet of cold water spurted from the shower head. With the shower spraying on Denis's bare chest, June pulled his head back a little further and whispered, "This will be our little secret Denis," and pointed the spray of cold water onto his face.

The force of the cold water made him struggle to move his head away from the spray, but June held it firm. His whole body started to shake and he was starting to gasp for breath. The urge to continue with her water torture was tempting but June didn't want him dead just yet. She released her grip on his hair and knocked the tap settings back to normal. As she turned off the running water the sound of her victim coughing and gasping for breath brought a smile to her face.

June grabbed the remote pad and pressed the button to raise the bathlift from the water. Denis's skin was covered with "goose bumps" and his whole body was trembling as he emerged from the soapy water.

Looking down at his skinny body she glanced at his tiny shrivelled penis. Grabbing it in her hand and squeezing it tightly she whispered in his ear, "To think you caused so much misery with this...this pathetic little prick. You really enjoyed sticking it where it didn't belong didn't you Denis."

She squeezed it even harder. Looking into his eyes she could see the pain she was causing him and it was exciting her.

"Can you imagine what it was like to have this disgusting thing forced into my mouth? Well, can you Denis? Can you imagine what it felt like to gag on your prick? No, I don't suppose you can. Well try this." As she finished taunting him her hand released his penis and grabbed his jaw, forcing his mouth open. She pushed two fingers of her other hand into his mouth, forcing them to the back of his throat, making him choke.

"And that doesn't even come close to it," she snapped.

Maureen was just entering the room as June removed her hands away from his face.

"I'll let you take over now. We've been getting on like a house on fire. Haven't we Denis?"

June walked out of the room not looking back. As she strolled down the corridor her friend could hear her singing, "First I was afraid, I was petrified..."

The two women kept a distance between them for the rest of the morning, only meeting up in the staff kitchen. As they were not alone in the kitchen both made banal conversation about the weather and television until there was just the two of them left. Both women sat in the comfort of an armchair clutching mugs of tea when Maureen quietly whispered to her friend.

"How did you get on? Did you have enough time with him?"

"Mmmm .I could happily have finished him off this morning but I've not had my pound of flesh yet. What state was he in after I left?" June said softly.

"He was bloody frozen to the bone. I don't want to know what you did but you upset him big style. His teeth or what's left of them were chattering as I dried him off. There was no expression on his face either. He looked to be in a trance."

June ended the conversation with, "Good. We'd better get back to work."

Maureen took the hint that her friend had no wish to discuss the matter further. June had not needed to put the needle and pliers to good use but there would be other days.

113

Chapter 29

June was awake bright and early the following morning. Monday had been a most rewarding day for her. She could still feel the buzz that had stayed with her since she had given Denis a bath he would never forget. Before finally settling down to sleep that night, June's mind had been in overdrive as she lay awake thinking of all the awful things she could do to him. She now held the power to destroy him slowly and painfully and it excited her.

Her next move would have to be low key as she needed him to recover from his invigorating bath. Her subconscious mind had been at work as she slept and a thought had popped into her head on waking. She allowed herself a few moments to stretch her stiff limbs and clear the sleep from her blurry eyes before rising and setting about planning her next little surprise for Denis.

June jumped out of bed and reached for her favourite bath robe. She loved the feel of the robe wrapped around her. Many nights had been spent in her robe and nightie, stretched out on her sofa watching television. It had become her "comfort blanket" in times of stress. Today she was not stressed, just excited. Coffee was what she needed to help engage her brain into gear at the start of what was hopefully going to be another eventful day for a certain old man.

Mixed emotions were running rife, faster than she could deal with them. Excitement was making her heart race a little faster and it was a sensation she was enjoying. She felt alive, a feeling that had previously evaded her. Her excitement was caused by the suffering of another person and her job was to take care of those most vulnerable. Hurting another human being was not in her nature. But there was one person she needed to hurt, needed him to feel some of the fear and pain he had inflicted on her. *Did two wrongs make a right? Did it make her as bad as Denis or even worse?* If it did, she would deal with the consequences later. But he had to suffer and that was not open to negotiation.

Two cups of coffee later and June was fully awake. She left the kitchen and headed back into her bedroom. Quickly, she shook her duvet and tidied up her bed then walked over to the chest of drawers that housed her underwear. One drawer also housed something that she had never wanted to put on display. Tucked away at the back of the top drawer was a vibrator, still in the original packaging. The plastic penis had been a prize that she had the misfortune to win at an Ann Summers party a few years earlier. If ever there was a more unsuitable prize to be won, that was it.

Holding the distasteful object in her hand brought back memories of the night Rita Kemp had held a party to promote flimsy nighties and other erotic objects. June would have rather walked over broken glass than spend an evening fondling strange looking gadgets that required a couple of batteries. But, Maureen had been insistent that they both went along for the laugh and even hinted that she may invest in something to put a smile on her face. As there was no way June could get out of going to the party she had painted a smile on her face and braced herself for some vulgarity and saucy female humour.

By the time the Ann Summers demonstrator had got out her bag of overpriced bits of lace and unusual looking gadgets, the guests had consumed plenty of cheap plonk and were already becoming rowdy and rude.

June's mother would have turned in her grave at just hearing the language that had been freely used. What would she have thought of her daughter participating in such vulgarity? One woman had been more than happy to disclose to everyone that her husband was very well endowed. What she had actually said was, "He can make my bloody eyes water sometimes when he goes at it at twenty to the dozen. And he's still got a an inch or two to spare!"

June had not needed to know such a fact and had prayed she would not be asked about her pathetic sex life with Nigel.

After a few too many glasses of cheap vino Maureen had lost any inhibitions she may have had and ordered herself a vibrator. Not content with a basic model she had been persuaded to invest in an all singing, all dancing deluxe version that was too much like the real thing for June's liking.

So, when June had the misfortune of winning a silly game of pass the parcel and removed the final sheet of wrapping paper, it had been more than she bargained for when her prize was revealed. Her first thought had been, *What am I going to do with a bloody vibrator?*

She had seen more than her fair share of male genitalia whilst working at Field Hall, even if most of them had resembled something that had shrivelled up and died. Hell would freeze over before she went to another such party she had promised herself.

A smile came to June's face as she remembered the reactions of all her fellow party goers when Rita delivered their erotic purchases to work a couple of weeks later. The look on Maureen's face when she saw the size of her new "best friend" was priceless. What had seemed like titillating toys when drunk, all appeared to be instruments of torture when viewed sober. The raunchy party girls had turned into shrinking violets as they mused over their purchases.

Memories of that party made her shudder but looking at the offending object in her hand, June decided it was time to put it to good use. Stripping it from the packaging she held the plastic penis in her palm.

"I know just the place for you," she said out loud and walked over to her freshly ironed tunic which was hanging in her wardrobe. She tucked the vibrator deep into the pocket then headed towards the bathroom to have a shower.

Washed, dressed and ready to go, June zipped up her black quilted jacket and tied a fluffy white scarf around her neck. It was a frosty Tuesday morning but she was hoping that things would hot up in more ways than one later in the day. Maureen was on time as usual and the friends met up for their daily amble to work. Maureen started their first conversation of the day by asking a question.

"Do you have any plans for you know who today?"

"I've got a little something to hand if the opportunity presents itself," June replied in a matter of fact way.

"Am I better off not knowing what the little something is?"

116

"Let's just say that I plan to give him a fucking mouthful!"

"Well...let's leave it at that!" Maureen sensed an air of determination and anger in her friends vulgar reply and changed the subject to the previous night's television viewing.

Chapter 30

Maureen Jones had started to feel the impact of her friend's quest for revenge. She fully understood her determination to seek revenge and supporting her entirely. But, since volunteering to watch June's back and even giving her opportunities to be alone with Denis, Maureen had not been able to get a decent night's sleep. She didn't want her friend to be caught dishing out rough justice and if she was to be honest, Denis would be doing her a favour if he just died. For someone so frail he was not succumbing to June's attempts at destroying him. *Just bloody die Denis, just die*, was the predominant thought she kept having.

There was to be another new resident arriving at Field Hall that day. Another room had become vacant. The poor chap with dementia had become very irritated and aggressive. A place had been found elsewhere which specialised in caring for Alzheimer sufferers. That was the end of Wee Willie Winkie's nocturnal wandering of the corridors at Field Hall. There was to be a new kid on the block.

On hearing that news June hoped that the new admission would be enough of a distraction to the staff to give her an opportunity to get Denis alone again.

Denis was still choosing to spend most of his time in the privacy of his room. His speech was still nothing more than grunts and groans though some members of the staff had noticed he was becoming more nonverbal and resorting to responding with head movements. Some had even commented that he was becoming more withdrawn and could be losing the will to live. It was a common reaction seen in the frail and weary and staff members were used the signs. Little did anyone know that Denis was beginning to wish he was dead.

Lunch had been served in the dining room, which was almost full that day. Again, Denis was not one of the diners tucking into meat and potato pie with all the trimmings, followed by rice pudding. He was obviously dining alone in his room.

June was keeping a careful eye on the comings and goings down the corridor leading to his room. Maureen was keeping a careful eye on her friend.

When most of the diners had finished eating June decided it would be safe to strike and casually announced to anyone within earshot, "I'll go see how poor Denis is. Better make sure he eats something before it goes cold."

Maureen was one of those in close proximity and had felt her heart miss a beat when she heard what June had said. She caught sight of her friend heading off towards Denis's room and took a deep breath. She said a silent prayer, *If you're listening God, please don't let her be caught.* Her nerves were making her feel jittery and she felt a sudden bowel movement coming on.

June lightly knocked on the door of number five, stepped just inside the room and asked, "Hello Denis love. Have you finished your lunch?"

She didn't give a toss if hadn't eaten a thing. The feigned concern was there to allay any suspicions if she was unexpectedly spotted entering his room.

Denis was sat in his armchair, his lunch was on a table beside him and the food had been barely touched. As he looked across at the figure standing just inside his room his face drained of colour. He had fear written all over his face and seeing his expression made June's pulse race. The powers that be appeared to be working in her favour. Denis had the television on. It would drown out some of the noise she may make.

June walked slowly over to the armchair and perched on the edge of the bed next to the scared old man.

"Now then Denis, do you remember me yet?"

There was no response to her question.

She picked up a desert spoon and scooped up a large dollop of rice pudding.

"Open wide for this lovely pudding Denis. We can't have you wasting away."

He still didn't reply or respond to her request.

"I said open wide you stupid old sod."

As she snapped angrily at him her hand grabbed his jaw and forced his mouth to open. She pushed the brimming spoonful of rice into his mouth and deposited it onto his tongue.

June was getting very slick with her hand movements and in a split second she had dropped the spoon and reached into the pocket of her tunic. In her hand she now had the vibrator and started rubbing it across Denis's lips.

"I asked you yesterday if you had any idea what it was like to have your disgusting prick forced into my mouth. Well, you're about to find out."

She rammed the vibrator as far into his mouth as possible, forcing some of the rice pudding to the back of his throat.

"What does it feel like Denis?" she asked as she thrust the vibrator back and forth as if simulating oral sex.

"Remember me yet? Remember any of the innocent kids you scarred with your fucking evil ways?"

The old man's face was turning puce and his eyes were bulging slightly as he struggled and tried to gasp for air. June knew she had to stop or he would choke, but her heart wanted her to carry on and on.

She pulled the vibrator out of his mouth allowing him to draw a breath. The remains of the rice pudding stuck to it so June wiped it down the front of the old man's jumper. She picked up a paper napkin from the table and threw it at him.

"Wipe your mouth you disgusting piece of shit. If you think that was bad well let me tell you now, it's not the last you'll see of this!"

She taunted him as she held up the eight inch plastic penis in front of his watery eyes as she wiped it clean with another serviette.

As Denis coughed, trying to clear his throat, June replaced the vibrator back in her pocket. Picking up the dishes and cutlery she walked towards the door. She could hear him gasping for breath as she opened the door to leave.

"I'll get you a nice cup of tea Denis. That's a nasty cough you've got there."

She closed the door behind her and sauntered back down the corridor.

Maureen breathed a sigh of relief when she saw June entering the dining room with the dirty dishes in her hand and sidled up to her as she was placing the crockery onto the trolley.

"Is he still breathing?"

"He was when I left him. Will you take him a cup of tea and check on him please," she whispered without moving her lips.

"Bloody hell, I hope he's not snuffed it. I don't want to be the one that finds him," Maureen muttered. Her heart was racing and her hands had started to tremble as she poured a mug of tea for someone she hoped was still alive and kicking.

Maureen's hands were shaking so badly she could barely keep the tea in the mug as she knocked on Denis's door and walked in. For one split second she thought the body slumped in the armchair was dead and almost stopped breathing herself. Then it moved and a pale old face looked at her through moist eyes.

"I've brought you a mug of tea Denis."

Even though she knew what a vile man he was she couldn't help but feel a little compassion for the frail shell of a human being. Oh how she wished she had never walked in his room on that fateful day. *Ignorance really can be bliss*, she thought.

It was Maureen's job to attend to the resident's needs and tend to them she would. She helped him hold the special mug so he could drink the tea he needed to clear his throat. The smears of rice pudding on his clothing were obvious. So thinking he had spilled it down himself she suggested changing his jumper. Denis nodded and made a faint throaty groan in response.

Looking closely at the old man's face as she helped him put on a clean jumper, Maureen tried to imagine what he would have looked like forty years ago. The evil, leering eyes that her friend had feared so much, eyes that had lusted after innocent children, were almost colourless now and lacking any spark of life. If she had not known about Denis's prison record she would have found it hard to believe he could commit such disgusting acts. Then, she remembered her sister was one of those innocent children he had preyed on.

121

Maureen took a reality check on her conflicting emotions and decided June was right. He deserved no sympathy.

"Right, drink your tea," she said very abruptly, then turned and walked out of his room without looking back.

The two friends had deliberately tried to avoid each other for the rest of their shift, apart from a brief exchange of looks and a sly nod of the head to let June know that Denis was still breathing. Maureen was bursting with curiosity to know what unpleasantness had been inflicted upon their resident paedophile. As soon as the pair were out of the building and out of earshot from other staff members she could contain herself no longer.

"What the hell did you do to him? I really thought he was a goner when I took him that tea. To put it bluntly, I nearly shit myself today. I'm a bloody nervous wreck. My hands are still shaking."

"I gave him a taste of his own medicine."

June went on to describe her actions and how close she came to finishing him off. She saw the look on Maureen's face and quipped "You did ask!"

"Where did you get a vibrator from anyway? I didn't have you down for that sort of thing."

"I won it at that rotten Ann Summers party! You can't have forgotten that night, you bought that monster of a thing. I finished up taking home a Pocket Rocket, as you named it. And while we're on the subject, did you ever actually try it out?" June was swift to reply.

She had often wondered what fate had become the deluxe dildo.

"Let's just say that our bedroom walls are not that thick and when it's turned on it sounds like a bloody pneumatic drill. I'd die of shame if either of my lads knew I had one," Maureen replied coyly.

"But have you actually ever given it a go?" June was determined to keep up the interrogation.

"Once!"

"And?"

"Okay, once or twice when the lads have been out. Well it's not the same as being with my Jack but it can certainly bring a smile to my face. Satisfied now?"

"I was just curious. I'm satisfied and you sound as if you were," June said with a chuckle in her voice. "Now let's forget about vibrators for one day. I'm ready for a stiff drink and a warm bath."

Chapter 31

Back home in the privacy of her kitchen, June opened her handbag and pulled out the vibrator still wrapped in a paper serviette. She had managed to make a quick visit to her locker shortly after leaving Denis's room and dispose of it in her bag. A couple of tissues had stopped the sticky residue of the rice pudding soaking through and making a mess of the bag's lining.

She ran the hot water tap over the offending object until the tissue had disintegrated and traces of rice and dried saliva had been flushed down the plug hole. Holding it in her hand, she remembered what her friend had confided in her on their walk home. *Could a lump of bobbly plastic and a couple of batteries put a smile on her face?* It wasn't as if she didn't have any sexual urges because she had wanted to do it with Nigel. It was always spoiled by flashbacks of her rape. Maybe when she had put Denis in a wooden box she would consider exploring her sexuality. Maybe....

After a lingering bath and wrapped in her comfort robe, June could feel the tensions of the day fading away. It hadn't been a particularly busy working day but all her cloak and dagger antics, scuttling in and out of Denis's room had made her feel edgy. A small part of her wanted it all to be over but she still hadn't got all the hate and anger out of her system.

Not in the mood for cooking, June decided on frozen pizza for supper and while she waited for it to cook she poured herself a glass of red wine. She savoured each soothing sip, her mind regressing back to her aggressive behaviour towards Denis Goodman. What humiliation could she inflict on him next?

She couldn't risk doing anything that affected his breathing again, it would have to be something painful. She knew exactly what she would like to do to him but doubted the opportunity would ever present itself. But, she would be ready if it ever did.

Chapter 32

Wednesday morning started out badly for June. Twice in the night she had woken up suddenly from dreams involving her evil uncle.

All the talk of vibrators from the previous day had preyed on her mind and become entangled with her dreadful memories. Denis had featured in her dreams once again.

She started her day full of a new loathing for him and an even stronger determination to inflict even more pain upon him. With anger raging inside her once again she decided to take the needle and pliers with her to work. It was time for more dentistry.

With only a couple of days to work before her next two day break, June knew she would have to make the most of every opportunity to torment her Nemesis. It was obvious his health had deteriorated since his arrival at Field Hall, probably due to her antics. If he was going to die, she was hell bent on being the cause. Risks would have to be taken.

"You look tired this morning." Maureen was being very observant for so early in the day.

June`s only response was a shrug of her shoulders.

"I`m surprised you can sleep at all. I`m turning into a bloody wreck just thinking about it all. Why can`t he just do us all a favour and croak?"

"No! He goes when I decide. He chose to come back here so I choose when he fucking leaves," June was quick to snap back at her friend in an unusually aggressive manner. Her excessive use of bad language did not go unnoticed.

Maureen had never seen this side of her friend`s personality before and was taken aback by her comments. If it had been anyone else who had been so quick to jump down her throat, she would have been equally as nasty and given them a verbal tongue lashing. Knowing what she did about June`s past, she was prepared to overlook her friends outburst and changed the topic of conversation quickly.

It wasn't only the weather that was frosty that morning as the pair walked the remainder of their short journey to work in silence. Turning into the drive leading up to Field Hall, Maureen said another silent prayer. *Please, please let him have died.*

There had been no mention of Denis at the morning meeting so the two women breathed a sigh of relief. He'd survived his ordeal. Maureen had felt the need to pop another Diacalm tablet to ease her jittery stomach.

But, there had been one bit of sad news announced that morning. Ivy Grimshaw who had been a resident for the past five years or so had passed away peacefully through the night. She had been well liked, even loved by some staff members for her kind nature and wicked sense of humour. Even at eighty five years old she had still enjoyed some friendly banter with everyone. Ivy would be sadly missed but there was no time for maudlin and her room would have to be prepared for a newcomer.

Ivy's room was down the same corridor as Denis's. That would mean a lot of comings and goings in that area and June realised she may be able to take advantage of poor Ivy's passing. As tired as she may have been earlier, her mind was now fully alert.

It took June by surprise to find Denis sat in the dining room that morning. He was in a wheelchair pushed up to a table with a dish of porridge in front of him. That set her thinking. *Was he suddenly finding a way of communicating better? Was he thinking he was safe from her if he sat in the communal rooms? Was he able to tell anyone of his ordeals?* June would have to watch and wait.

All morning she kept her distance from the old man avoiding all eye contact with him. Maureen had also spotted him and exchanged a knowing look with her friend when she saw him appearing to watch television in the sitting room. Both knew he couldn't sit there all day. Sooner or later he would need to use a toilet or be prepared to sit in his own mess. Either way, June would do her best to make sure she was around when he was ready to move. Bearing this fact in mind she made a dash to the staff cloakroom. She needed to dump the pliers and needle and replace them with something more appropriate for what she had in mind.

Her anger and hatred were now at boiling point. If Denis Goodman thought for one second that he was being a sly old fox then he was wrong. June was like a hound that had caught his scent and was ready to hunt him to his death.

Maureen could sense her friends agitated mood and was getting worried she may start to be careless. It had seemed a long morning. Trying to concentrate on looking after the other residents while keeping a watchful eye on Denis and June had Maureen stressed out. She was so relieved when it was time for a lunch break.

The two women usually took their breaks together and for a short time she would be able to relax, knowing exactly what her friend was doing.

The atmosphere in the staff room was very subdued that day. The other members of the staff were mourning the death of Ivy Grimshaw and were oblivious to the tension between the two anxious friends.

Maureen sat quietly eating a sandwich while her friend sat opposite clutching a mug of coffee. June reminded her of a coiled snake, ready to rear up and strike at any time. Whatever she had in mind to do, it was obvious that nothing and no one was going to stop her.

Another silent prayer was offered up to God, any god that would listen. *Please don't let her be caught.*

Any conversations that had taken place in the staff room during their break had been about Ivy and her funeral arrangements. June had not contributed in any way. She had just sat silent throughout.

If God was granting wishes, it was June's wish that was granted that day. As the friends left the staff room and were heading back into the resident's dining room Denis Goodman was being wheeled out.

Joanne Dixon, one of the younger and newer members of the team was pushing his wheelchair. June saw an opportunity and was going to seize it with both hands; literally.

"Isn't it your lunch break Joanne? Go on, have your break. I'll see to Denis. We're big mates now aren't we Denis?" June insisted.

"Well...if you're sure you don't mind. Thanks," Joanne replied gratefully. "He's had lunch but he needs the toilet."

June stepped behind the wheelchair and was heading off towards room number five before Joanne had a chance to change her mind.

Maureen's heart sank to the floor.

Entering the room backwards June pulled the wheelchair inside, spun it round and closed the door with her elbow. Her heart was racing so fast she felt dizzy with an adrenalin rush. Her hands were shaking but this was her moment and nothing was going to stop her.

She wheeled the chair towards the bed, stopped and put on the brakes.

"Stand up Denis. I need to undo your trousers," she ordered.

He remained sitting and turned his head away.

"Stand up!" she demanded.

Still he refused to move. June reached across to the bedside cabinet and grabbed the television remote pad and turned it on. She needed some background noise and turned the volume up a couple of notches.

"I said stand up. Now stand or I'll drag you out of that chair!" She reached out to grab his arms as he turned to look at her.

"Stand up. It's pointless trying to fight me Denis. I'm the strong one now. You're the helpless victim and you will do as I say. Remember, this is our little secret. Do you know who I am yet? I'll jog your memory. Now stand up!"

She could see defeat written on his face as he placed his left hand on the arm of the chair. June grabbed both of his arms and pulled him up.

"Rest your good arm on the bed while I unfasten your trousers!"

He didn't make a sound as June unbuttoned the waist band, pulled down the zip and yanked his trousers down to his knees, exposing his well washed underpants. She could also see the top of the special stretchy briefs that held his incontinence pad in place.

"Still wearing a nappy are we Denis? Don`t you think it`s strange that the parts that gave you so much pleasure are now causing you so much trouble?"

As she spoke, her hands grabbed both pairs of underpants at the waist and in one swift tug they were also round his knees exposing his bare buttocks. The soreness surrounding his anal opening was obvious. It was a nappy rash probably caused by excessive scratching.

If he had been any other male resident June would have been full of sympathy and done her best to ease his discomfort. But this wasn`t any other man and sympathy for him was non- existent. Instead she put her left hand on the back of his head and forced it down onto the bed. His left arm was stretched out across the bed and his useless right arm lay limp down his side.

"What does it feel like Denis to be so afraid? I don`t remember you showing me any sympathy and compassion when you were gratifying your disgusting needs. Remember me yet? I`ll give you a clue. Who was your loving, trusting niece?"

A faint moan was muffled as she pushed his face even harder onto the bed.

"Do I detect your memory is coming back? Yes, I`m little June, the little girl who loved her favourite uncle. Loved and trusted him. But you betrayed my trust Denis. You didn`t love me, you just wanted to use me to satisfy your perverted urges. You are one fucking sick bastard. Oh, I know you were in prison. How many more little girl`s lives did you ruin? Did you like little boys as well? Fuck you Denis! Fuck you!"

Holding his head firmly to the bed, June reached into her pocket with her right hand and continued to taunt him.

"When you were in prison did you satisfy your needs on other inmates? Or were you someone else`s fuck? Did you take it up the arse Denis? You`ve tried everything else so why not eh? Yes, a sick bastard like you knows no boundaries. Can you remember what it felt like to have a prick up your arse Denis? Let me remind you."

One quick move of her hand and June had pulled out the vibrator that had nearly choked him previous day. Wasting no time, she forced it between his buttocks and into his anal opening. His body jerked as she pushed the vibrator further inside him, inch by inch.

"Is that nice Denis? Would you like a bit more? There`s a couple more inches still to go. You`re moaning Denis. Is that with ecstasy? I remember you moaning as you took your pleasure from me. Don`t expect me to stop now. You`re going to find out just how it was for me when you forced your dirty prick inside me." June`s pot of anger had well and truly boiled over. She could hold back no longer.

"I remember the feeling Denis. I`ve never stopped feeling it. Never! You took away more than my virginity, you took away everything. You ruined my life. Did you show me any compassion? No, never. You reap what you sow in this world and you were happy to sow your seeds in me."

June pulled out the vibrator, leaving about an inch still inside him, then thrust it all back inside with a vengeance. Another muffled groan came from him as his body jerked again.

"I can`t stop now Denis. You must know that. You couldn`t stop when you were fucking me could you?"

As she spoke she continued to push the vibrator in and out, in and out, repeating "Fuck you!" with each thrust.

It was the sight of blood on the vibrator that was the warning she needed to make her stop.

She pulled the eight inches of plastic from his body and released her grip on his head. Traces of fresh blood covered it`s surface mixed with small specks of excrement.

June ran to the bathroom and grabbed the roll of toilet paper, pulling off sheet after sheet. The toilet paper absorbed all the mess and she flushed it down the toilet. More sheets were wrapped around the vibrator before she rammed it back into her pocket. There was no time to wash her hands before returning to the bedroom.

The sight of Denis sprawled across the bed, buttocks fully exposed showing a small trickle of blood running down to his inner thigh didn`t faze her. She had stripped him of his dignity and had no feelings of remorse.

The old man stayed silent but she could hear him breathing heavily. His body felt limp as she pulled up his underwear and then his trousers, leaning over his body to fasten the button and pull up the zip.

"Get up Denis. You're not dead yet but I bet you wish you were. I often wished I was dead after you had fucked me," she said in her normal tone of voice. "Now, let's get you back in the chair."

She scooped her arms under his belly to pull his torso into an upright position. Holding him close to her she managed to get him upright.

"Now sit back down in your wheelchair and keep your mouth shut. Remember, this is our little secret."

He flopped down into the chair. His legs hadn't the strength to keep him upright.

Maureen had been anxiously watching and waiting for her friend to come out of Denis's room. When it been almost ten minutes and June had still not come out she feared her friend may have done something seriously silly. Not wanting to get involved, Maureen was in a quandary. Should she risk her job or help her friend?

Her decision was to wander up the corridor and listen at the door. If anyone saw her she would have to say she was looking for June to give her a message. No one would question her actions. So off she went with her heart pounding so loud it was deafening her.

As Maureen stopped outside room number five it was eerily quiet. She was just debating with herself as to whether she should enter or not when the door opened. June was pulling the wheelchair out of the room with Denis sat in it. Relief swept over Maureen at the sight of the old man. He was still alive at least.

"I wondered where you had got to. Thought you might need a bit of help with Denis," Maureen lied.

"We're fine aren't we Denis? But, could you do me a favour and take him back to the day room? I need to have a word with the nurse about Denis," June asked her friend in her usual calm manner.

"Yes, course I will."

Maureen took control of the wheelchair and set off down the corridor giving her friend strange, questioning looks as they walked.

Denis's chair was parked up so he had a good view of the flat screen television in the corner of the day room. Members of the staff were unaware that he had not been to the toilet as planned and assumed he was happy to watch the day time programmes.

The old man sat in the wheelchair had no interest in what was going on around him. All he was aware of was the fact he had a throbbing pain inside him and had wet himself. He was very uncomfortable and wanted to return to his room and to his bed where he could hide away from everyone. All he could concentrate on were the questions he was asking himself. Now he knew why he had been hurt, humiliated and shamed. *Was having a stroke and being left with a useless body punishment for his sins? What did she plan on doing to him next?* He wished he was dead.

After a sneaky visit to the cloakroom to dump any incriminating evidence June had found Sarah Stead the duty nurse, writing up some reports at the reception desk. Sarah was one of three fully qualified nurses who were responsible for administering the resident's medication.

If any other members of the staff had any concerns or noticed any changes in a resident's mood or general health their observations were recorded. June wanted to report something about the state of a certain old man's health.

"Hi Sarah, have you got a minute?"

"Sure. What's up?"

"I've just taken Denis Goodman to the toilet and I think he may be constipated. He might have piles as well. He had trouble passing a stool and there was a bit of fresh blood present. He's got a bit of a sore rash as well. I've asked him if he's had any pain before but he can't or won't answer. How much of it is the after effect of his stroke and how much is him being awkward, I just don't know. At best he just waves his hand. I thought you might be able to give him something to soften the stools."

"Where is he now?"

"He's back in the day room."

"I'll check him over when I've finished this. Is he eating properly?"

"I don't think he is. I've tried to get him to eat more on a few occasions but he just doesn't seem interested. I don't think he wants to be here. In fact, I don't think he wants to be anywhere. He's wasting away. I'm surprised he has come out of his room today. He's been a bit of a recluse."

"Right, leave it with me. I'll see what I can do. My next job is to sort out the repeat prescriptions orders. I can ask them to prescribe something for him."

"That's fine. Thank you Sarah."

June was feeling smug at the thought of him being poked and prodded all over again by the nurse. Her anger was fading but not entirely gone. She knew exactly what would make her anger disappear and that would be the disappearance of Denis Goodman into a wooden box.

She returned to the day room and immediately Maureen asked, "What are you up to?"

She was sensing June was feeling very smug about something. She received no verbal reply, just a tap of June's nose with her index finger and a wink of an eye. To which, Maureen raised her eyes to the ceiling and shrugged her shoulders.

About an hour later just as she had promised, Sarah was seen wheeling Denis out of the day room. Maureen shot a questioning glance at June to which she just smiled.

"You can tell me later, if my nerves can stand the suspense."

"You might just wish you'd never asked," was June's reply.

Maureen was still shaking her head slowly at that comment as she walked over to offer her arm as a support to one of the female residents, struggling to get up out of a chair. She had a feeling it was going to be a long afternoon.

Denis never returned to the television room for the rest of the day after being taken away by the nurse.

June waited until her shift was coming to an end before enquiring about him to Sarah Stead.

"Was I right about Denis?" she asked, trying to sound concerned.

"I'm going to ask for a visit from his doctor tomorrow. He was obviously in some discomfort when I examined him and there was some blood on the pad he had on. Probably piles but I'd better get him looked at," Sarah informed her.

June nodded her approval struggling to stop her face breaking into a big smile. The doctor would give Denis an internal inflicting a little more discomfort upon him. Never in a million years would a doctor consider the bleeding to be caused by a vibrator. She felt sure her actions would go undetected and even if Denis could speak he wouldn't want the truth coming out about his seedy past.

Would Maureen really want to know what had gone on behind the closed door of room number five? Perhaps? Once she knew would it change their relationship? June was about to find out.

"I know I might regret asking, but what's been going on?" Maureen's curiosity was getting the better of her. The two women had only reached the end of the drive before she had started her interrogation.

"If you want the whole truth then fine, but not here. Come to mine and you can have a blow by blow account. But you have been warned. Today I was out to make him pay. He knows exactly who I am now."

"I think I'm up to my neck in it already. So, in for a penny as the saying goes. Let's get that kettle on."

Maureen had made her decision and linked her arm through her friend's in gesture of support. They walked the rest of their short journey to June's flat linked arm in arm in comfortable silence.

Chapter 33

"I don't know about putting the kettle on, I need something a bit stronger. Do you fancy a glass of wine?" June asked, as the pair kicked off their shoes in the hallway.

"I've got a sinking feeling that I'm going to need more than a glass, but it'll do for starters." Maureen was bracing herself for June's confession.

Clutching their wine glasses in hand, the two friends settled down on the sofa. June was the first to take a large mouthful and give a big sigh of relief as the red wine warmed her throat. Maureen followed suit but gulped down two large mouthfuls before she felt the kick in her throat. Both women were feeling the strains of the day for completely different reasons.

"I think I'm ready to hear the worst now," Maureen sighed.

"Well, here goes."

June started to reveal the details of how she had seized the opportunity to be alone with Denis. Feeling calm and relaxed made it far more difficult for her to express the anger and hatred that had driven her to perform the depraved act she had inflicted on a helpless old man. Describing how she had felt as she had rammed the vibrator in and out of his body was almost impossible to do. Only a person who had been raped could and would understand the anger. It wasn't all about inflicting pain it was shame what she wanted Denis Goodman to feel. She prayed her friend would understand that she had to have her pound of flesh if she was ever to put the past behind her once and for all.

When June had finished confessing her sins she turned to face her friend, expecting to see a look of disapproval to say the least. Maureen's face had a solemn expression giving no clue as to her feelings. And then she spoke.

"Where's the vibrator now?"

"In my handbag. Why?"

"Do you have a hammer?"

"Under the kitchen sink. Why?"

Her friend was avoiding answering her questions. Maureen put her wine glass down onto the glass topped coffee table and eased herself up from the comfort of the sofa and walked into the kitchen. She remained silent as she opened the kitchen sink cupboard door and searched for a hammer amongst the bottles of washing up liquid and an array of other cleaning products. The small hammer was behind the numerous containers just as June had said.

With the hammer clutched in her hand she returned to the living room and walked over to the dining table where June's handbag had been hastily dumped. Still remaining silent, Maureen opened up her friend's bag and pulled out an object covered in toilet paper. She knew from the shape alone that what she was holding was the vibrator or has she had called it, the pocket rocket.

June looked on in total confusion as her friend grabbed a magazine from off of the coffee table and threw it onto the carpet. Maureen kneeled down and placed the vibrator on to the magazine. She looked up at June, raised her hand with the hammer firmly gripped in it and smashed it down hard, striking the paper covered object. Two more hard blows followed in quick succession. Within seconds the vibrator had been reduced to bits, still covered in toilet paper.

Maureen finally said, "Now you see it, now you don't. Stick this mess into your bin."

June did as her friend had asked and scooped up the magazine and tipped the lot into her waste bin.

"Now what were you saying about poor Denis having a dose of the Farmer Giles? It's not surprising is it when he eats so little. He needs a bit of roughage in his diet. I'm sure his doctor will get him sorted. Is there a drop more wine in the bottle chuck?" Maureen asked as she flopped back down onto the sofa and picked up her glass.

The wine bottle was empty but the friends were happy to share the remains of a bottle of sherry that June had found tucked away in her sideboard.

Maureen finally left her friend's flat feeling a little merry from drinking on an empty stomach. But, before June opened the door to let her friend out she had one last thing to say.

"I know you've not finished with him yet but please be careful June. I'll be watching your back."

With those words of caution, Maureen wobbled out of the door and set out on her short walk home.

June closed and locked the door, raised her eyes to look up at the ceiling and whispered "Thank you God."

Chapter 34

Thursday morning dawned and June could tell it was another chilly and frosty one before she got out of bed. The central heating had already kicked on. Her head was throbbing slightly from the mix of wine and sherry that she had consumed. Sherry always gave her a bad head and that was why it had been pushed to the back of the sideboard. But, the previous evening had been an exceptional one and both women had needed a drink.

As it was the last day of that week`s shifts, June had decided to have a break from tormenting Denis. If a visit from his doctor was on the cards then there would be no windows of opportunity to get him alone. Another internal examination from the doctor would be enough to make his eyes water and just knowing that was enough to make her laugh.

June started to think about the planned visit from a doctor. *Just which G.P. practice had Denis registered with? Had he returned to the area and gone back to his old surgery? Had he been accepted there? If he had, that would mean Denis was a patient at the same surgery as she was.* It was very doubtful that any of the staff at the surgery would have been working there long enough to remember him. Denis had been a patient in the early 1970`s. She was convinced that whichever doctor turned up that day would not make any connection between her and her uncle. As a precaution she would make herself scarce when he or she turned up at Field hall.

Other thoughts had been niggling at her for days. *Just how long had Denis been living in the area before he had his stroke? Weeks? Years? How long had he been out of prison exactly? What address had he been living at? Why had he returned to his hometown? Had he hoped to find his sister was still living in the area? Did he know she had died?* And then there was the sixty four thousand dollar question. *Had he made enquiries about June and where she was now*? There was something just not right about Denis's return to Burtley.

Maureen looked very pale in the face when the friends met just outside June's flat. She was muffled up in a thick maroon quilted coat and fluffy black scarf around her neck that made her skin look almost grey. Two dark circles under her eyes completed the unflattering panda look.

"You look rough!" was June's greeting to her sickly looking friend.

"Rough is not the word I'd use. That bloody sherry has given me a right throbbing head. I could have had a duvet day today, believe me."

"Get a cup of strong coffee and a couple of painkillers. You'll be fighting fit in no time. And...I'm not planning on paying a certain old man a visit to day, so you can relax," June reassured her weary mate.

"Well you'll have to make it because I could chuck up for tuppence and anyway you don't look so perky yourself!" Maureen snapped back.

The two women were met at the entrance to the drive of Field Hall by Sarah Stead, the nurse who had decided Denis should be seen by a doctor. They exchanged a few comments about the cold weather on the short walk up to the front door and then parted company. As Sarah headed off in the opposite direction June muttered very quietly to her friend, "I'm going to make myself scarce when the doctor calls, so don't panic if you don't see me for a while. I don't want Sarah calling me to discuss with the doctor what I reported to her about Denis. I'm just praying that the bleeding is thought to be piles and constipation."

Maureen had managed to gulp down a cup of coffee and swallow a couple of pills before the morning meeting started. June had also taken a couple of pills with her drink to ease the dull ache at the back of her head that had been steadily getting worse. Neither women had much enthusiasm in what was being reported until Denis's name was mentioned. Then their headaches were instantly forgotten.

A member of the night staff had also brought it to the attention of the night nurse that Denis still had some rectal bleeding. A doctor's visit was on the cards for him and a couple of other residents who were suffering with flu type symptoms.

June had felt a tightening in her chest at the mention of rectal bleeding but dare not pry as to how bad it actually was. Had she done some irreparable damage to him?

Fortunately, two other staff members made comments about Denis`s poor diet and the fact that he had suffered with bouts of diarrhoea recently. It was going to be a long and stressful morning for June, waiting for the doctor to make his diagnosis.

Poor Maureen was also feeling anxious about the doctor`s visit. What had her friend done to him?

Knowing that doctors do routine visits after their morning surgeries, June knew approximately what time she should start to keep a low profile. From eleven thirty onwards she was on red alert.

Once a month a couple of musicians came to Field Hall as part of the activity programme. Bringing a keyboard along with them and a selection of percussion instruments, a husband and wife duo sang and played songs from the war era and many other old favourites. The residents were encouraged to join in and have a good old sing song, which was always enjoyed by all who took part.

Bingo was played at intervals and this was the opportunity that June had been banking on. Some of the less agile or partially sighted needed help marking off the numbers on their bingo cards. She would busy herself with helping out wherever she could and until the entertainment started in the afternoon there would be lunch to serve and assist with. That would keep her busy enough for a few hours.

It was an Asian male doctor who visited Field Hall that day. June had managed to keep having a crafty peep out of the dining room across to the reception desk. Whoever the doctor was, she was sure he had not come from the surgery she was registered at.

It had taken less than twenty minutes for the doctor to see all three ailing residents. June heard the nurse, Sarah Stead, thanking him for visiting as he breezed through the reception area and out of the front door. Sarah had a fistful of prescription sheets in her hand. June needed to know if there was a prescription for Denis or if the doctor had thought his bleeding needed hospital treatment for further investigations. She had her fingers crossed it was the former and not the latter option.

First she had a session of cutting and chopping up plates of braising steak, Yorkshire puddings and vegetables and helping those who needed assistance with feeding to keep her occupied.

When everyone in the dining room had finished their meals, June decided to make her way to the staff toilets and casually, enquire en route, how Denis was. Drawing in a couple of deep breaths she sauntered towards the reception desk.

"Hi Sarah, how's Denis today? Did the doctor call?"

"Yes, he came a while ago. He tried to do a bit of an internal but Denis got worked up about it. He thinks it's probably his poor diet causing constipation. He's given him some suppositories and cream and prescribed a course of steroids to increase his appetite. He might be a bit less of a recluse if he can start to eat and put a bit of weight on. He's getting very frail." Sarah had given June the answers she had been praying for.

A rip roaring afternoon was spent singing along with the musical duo's rendering of songs from the war and playing bingo for the fantastic prize of a box of Maltesers. Bingo games seemed to take an eternity to complete when it took the residents two minutes to mark off each and every number. But June's afternoon passed peacefully and pleasantly enough.

When the Bingo machine was finally put away and the final chorus of "We'll meet again" had been cheerfully sung, June found herself thinking about Denis again. She had reassured her friend that today she would leave him alone but the urge to visit him was getting stronger by the minute. She was now wrestling with her conscience. Finally, her urge to see him won the battle over her promise to a friend.

About fifteen minutes before the end of her shift June sauntered over to the reception desk where the nurse was busy on the computer.

"Sarah, If anyone wants me I'm just going to look in on our sick banana's before I go home. I haven't had a chance to see them today and I'm off for a couple of days."

The sick banana's were Gladys and Irene who were confined to their beds with Flu symptoms and of course Denis.

"Okay." Sarah was too engrossed with whatever was on the computer monitor to even look up.

June's first port of call was Gladys Dearlove. Gladys was a nice eighty two year old lady who had been at Field Hall for the past couple of years. She gave a gentle knock on the door and walk in cheerfully asking, "Hello Gladys. How are you feeling? You'll soon be back on your feet. I'm off for a couple of days, so when I come back I expect to see you up and about."

Gladys smiled and muttered something that sounded like, "I will be."

Next for a visit was Irene Gilroy, another nice lady who was a close friend of Gladys. The two often spent time alone together in each other's rooms. Now both had caught the same virus. June said exactly the same to Irene as she had to Gladys and made her way down the corridor to room number five.

Gently she knocked at the door and slowly opened the door just far enough to poke her head around it. Denis looked towards the door. On seeing her face he looked away sharply.

"Hello Denis love. How are you?"

She spoke loud enough for anyone around to be able to hear.

"I just thought I'd call in to see how you are today."

Denis was in bed with the television on.

Closing the door behind her, June walked slowly over to his bed. Denis was looking away and avoiding having to look at her.

"It won't work Denis. I'm not going away. You must know by now that I'm going to make your life as miserable and as painful as I can. The best thing you could do for yourself now is die. Just die! It'll be much easier for us both."

As she finished speaking, with her left hand she grabbed his face and forced him to turn in her direction. Her right hand pulled back his sheet and duvet and then reached down to his groin. Forcing her hand down his pyjamas and the thin stretchy briefs he was wearing, she was able to feel his testicles and grabbed hold of them tightly.

She saw his face flinch as she tightened her hold on the small fleshy lumps.

"I'm told that a man's balls are most sensitive to pain and injury. Shall we see if it's true?" she whispered in his ear as her grip on him got tighter.

"I wonder just how painful it'll get if I twist them a bit."

His face was grimaced as she twisted her hand round and squeezed his balls as tightly as possible. He let out a moan, but June stifled the sound by covering his mouth with her hand.

"You're going to die Denis and it's going to be soon. I'm going to kill you, slowly and painfully. I want you out of my life. You should never have come back," she taunted him as her grip stayed strong.

"You have turned me into an evil monster, Denis. I'm like Dr. Jeckyl and Mr. Hyde since seeing you again. But you were the monster Denis. You! Not me."

With that threat she released her hand that had been gripping his groin, formed a fist and punched his testicles with great force. His response was a typical knee jerking reaction, pulling up his legs to his knees.

"Die Denis. Die!" With that command she turned and walked out of the room without looking back.

Behind the door of number five lay an old man in agonising pain, too weak to cry out. As tears trickle down his ashen face he realises that he was going to die and wishing he was already dead.

"Oh, there you are. I wondered where you had got to." Maureen was in the cloakroom putting on her coat when June walked in to join her.

"I dropped in on Gladys and Irene to see how they were."

Maureen instantly knew from June's body language that she was not being entirely truthful and there was only one reason for her to be so evasive. Denis Goodman.

Chapter 35

Friday 23rd March 2012

Maureen and June had arranged to meet at 1.00pm on Friday afternoon to attend Ivy Grimshaw's funeral. It was being held at the local crematorium, situated on the outskirts of Burtley. The couple had visited there far too many times for their liking, but it came as part of the job. Staff who were not on duty on the day of a deceased resident's funeral always attended to pay their respects. Occasionally other residents would also wish to go along and say their goodbyes to their dear departed friends. Today, it was just the two friends.

Punctual as always, Maureen was waiting outside the Co-op mini market in town at 1.00pm. She was anxious for her friend to arrive on time. She had some news that would interest June and wanted to tell her all about it before they got to the crematorium.

"Guess what our Graham has managed to find out now?" Maureen was bursting to tell her news.

"What? I'm not psychic so spill."

"He did a bit more delving into Denis Goodman's records and it seems he came back into the area about three years ago. His last known address was in York Road. It was a rented property and I'm sure they are all small terraced houses in that road. He wouldn't be able to live alone in a house after his stroke, so that'll be how he came to be with us," she blurted out without taking a breath.

"Well, now we know where he's been lurking but why come back to Burtley? He must have known I could still be living here. It makes no sense to me," June answered with a hint of anger in her voice.

June's mood could be detected in her gait. With her back straight and shoulders pulled back she took long strides as the couple set off walking in the direction of the crematorium. Poor Maureen having shorter legs was tottering alongside in her two inch heeled boots.

"Bloody hell June, slow down a bit. I'm knackered. I've only got little legs you know," her exhausted friend begged, after trying to keep up the pace for five minutes.

Slowing the pace down was easy but June's posture was still rigid. Her walk to the funeral was anything but a leisurely stroll as they had planned. Maureen knew something was bothering her friend and it wasn't just the news she had just delivered.

"You went in to see him again last night didn't you?"

"Yes!"

"Why? You said you wouldn't go near him. It was too risky. Too soon," Maureen asked, confused by her friend's odd behaviour.

"I don't know why. His very presence on this earth is getting to me. How long have you known me? Have I ever done anything to hurt anyone? No! Now, I can barely think of nothing else but hurting him and I know I won't stop until he's dead." There was anger and frustration in her voice.

Both women remained silent for the rest of their walk. On arrival at the crematorium both looked in sombre moods but it wasn't just the death of a much loved lady that was the cause.

They slowly followed Ivy's cortege inside and took their seats behind her grieving family, all of who's faces reflected June's low mood.

Some young male cleric was standing at the front of the small chapel reciting prayers and rambling on about Ivy having gone to a better place. June's thoughts were about someone else and not the deceased body laid out in the small pine coffin.

She realised she was being disrespectful to Ivy but just looking at the wooden box was making her wish she was at Denis's funeral. If it could only be him inside with the lid securely nailed down then she could go back to her normal life again. The day that his wooden box disappeared behind those red velvet curtains would be a day for celebration.

Then, another thought popped into her head. *What if he had made arrangements to have a burial? When would he have made such arrangements and with whom?* It was highly unlikely he had planned ahead. *But was that the reason he had returned to Burtley? Did he want to be laid to rest in his home town?* When he died, June wanted to be sure that his body and soul would be totally gone from this earth and not have to think that his rotting remains were somewhere in the local graveyard.

"You're thinking about him. I can tell," Maureen whispered as softly as she could in June's ear. "Give yourself a break. You're letting him take over your life again. Don't let him!"

June turned and gave her a forced smile as she felt a hand grasp hers and squeeze it gently in another show of genuine affection. Maureen's caring gesture brought tears to June's eyes as she held on tightly to her dearest and only friend.

"I'll try, I promise."

The short service was quickly over and as the mourners filed past Ivy's coffin it was obvious she had been loved by her weeping family members. June and Maureen also stopped at the coffin to silently say their goodbyes, before making their exit.

The small group of Ivy's family and friends were going to the local public house for the obligatory funeral buffet and refreshments. Invitations to attend had been accepted by both women who were feeling in need of something a little stronger than a cup of tea and a sausage roll.

The Coach and Horses public house had prepared a modest buffet for the wake. Maureen was one of the first to visit the usual spread of ham sandwiches, chicken legs and sausage rolls. The obligatory urn was bubbling alongside for those who only wished to mark Ivy's passing with a nice cup of tea.

"Not very imaginative buffet is it? I don't suppose her nearest and dearest will have wanted to splash out on much in case poor Ivy has not left much in her will. Assuming she had a will of course," she muttered from the corner of her mouth to June.

"Do I detect a hint of sarcasm there? You know what they say... Where there's a will there's a relative! It makes no difference to Ivy now anyway." June lifted her glass of lager and took a drink before continuing their conversation. "I wonder how many will turn out to his funeral?"

"I'm assuming you mean Denis. Who is there left in his family...other than you? He's not making any attempt to make friends with anyone either. Who foots the bill for the funeral if he snuffs it?" Maureen asked out of genuine interest.

"He's no relative of mine! And it's not if he snuffs it, the word you're looking for is when! He can have a paupers funeral, he's going to hell anyway so the sooner he goes into that oven the better." June took another drink from her lager. "I need another drink. Better make it a pint this time and it's your round."

Quite a few more pints were downed by the two friends before they left The Coach and Horses and walked their separate ways. June's previous straight back and long strides had given way to a much slower pace and a slight wobble in her steps.

Maureen continued to totter on her high heels aiming to walk in a straight line. Both women could feel their beds calling them.

Chapter 36

Saturday 24th March 2012

A dull ache was generating from the back of June's neck and spreading fast to her forehead and temples. She managed to open her eyes but simply looking around her bedroom was making her headache worse. Then the events of the previous day came flooding back to her. Her head throbbed even more.

She couldn't remember just how many pints of lager she had downed in The Coach and Horses but it was far more than was good for her. It had been a long time since she had suffered from a hangover. Then a hint of nausea swept over her causing cold sweat to cover her entire body.

Her mouth started to water, heralding a bout of vomiting and she knew that no matter how bad her headache was she needed to get out of bed and to her bathroom, pronto! There was no point in taking her time crossing the bedroom as she could feel the contents of her stomach already rising. She was going to make a mad dash and pray she reached the toilet before throwing up or passing out.

She made it to the bathroom just in time, dropping to her knees and hugging the toilet before parting with the entire contents of her stomach. Vomiting was bad enough but it was the dizziness and retching that she detested. But, she knew it had to be gone through before she could start to feel better.

After twenty minutes of hollering into the porcelain bowl between waves of dizziness, June finally felt she may be able to get up off of her knees. She still felt weak and her headache was unrelenting, but the sickness had passed. Silent vows were made as she clutched the bath side to steady herself.

"I will never get drunk again and I will never touch another drop of lager as long as I live."

About an hour later with a slice of toast, a cup of tea and two Paracetamol inside her, June was feeling about fifty percent normal.

She had made the decision to spend the rest of the day recovering; stretched out on her sofa, catching up on her favourite television programmes. Physically, she wasn't up to doing much more and the strain of having to deal with Denis Goodman back in her life was starting to tell.

It was 11.00am before June picked up her mobile and pressed Maureen's number on speed dial. Two hours had passed since she had been forced to dash out of bed and she was curious to know if her drinking partner was also suffering the after effects of too much lager.

"Hello." The voice on the other end of the call sounded croaky and weak, but June recognised her it as her friend's.

"Are you feeling as bad as me? I've been chucking up something rotten. Jesus, how many did we sink yesterday?"

"I'm as rough as chuff. I left my bloody head on the pillow this morning when I went to pray at the porcelain pot. Did you have your prayer mat out this morning? God knows what we drank but it was going down like nectar." Maureen sounded as weary and ill as her drinking buddy.

June blew out a big sigh before she replied, "Well I'm not moving from this sofa today. There's things I should be doing but they'll all have to wait. It's been a long, long time since I felt this bad. But we gave old Ivy a good send off."

"My head's banging and my stomach's singing to me. I'm doing nowt at all today. I might just go back to bed."

"Okay, I'll see you tomorrow morning, God willing. Bye." June pressed the button to halt her call. It may have been the power of suggestion, but another wave of nausea overcame her. She sprinted off on another visit to the bathroom to part with her breakfast.

It was almost 4.00pm in the afternoon when June finally started to feel human again. Her entire day had been spent making mad dashes to the loo. Finally she was able to look into her bathroom mirror and see some colour returning to her face.

Feeling so ill had totally taken her thoughts away from Denis Goodman for a few hours. Now she was returning to the human race, he was starting to drift back into her mind. His days were now

149

numbered and those days were not going to turn into weeks. For what remained of the day, June was going to concentrate on finalising her plans to finish him off, once and for all.

Stretched out on her sofa she allowed her thoughts to go to some dark places in her mind that she didn't even know existed. A certain person had come back and stirred up horrible memories. *How could she push Denis Goodman to the limit and make him breathe his last, without leaving any evidence of her actions?*

Various ideas came into her head but nothing that would let her walk away a free woman. Exhausted and still feeling weak, June drifted into a light sleep.

Her eyes opened wide and for a few seconds June could not get her thoughts together. Where was she and what day was it? Then her panic passed and reality was restored. While she had slept her subconscious mind had gone into overdrive and worked on her dilemma. Now she had what could be the solution to all her problems.

First thing June needed to do was boot up her laptop and do a little research before she could start to prepare for Denis's demise. The laptop that she had been so reluctant to purchase had been invaluable during the past weeks.

If by surfing the internet she could get the information she desperately needed, then her laptop had been worth far more than the few hundred pounds she had forked out for it. When she was deliberating in P.C. World with some spotty youth as to the benefits of owning a computer, she never envisaged needing to look up methods of how to kill someone. *What kind of a monster am I turning into?* June could not bring herself to answer that question.

The information she sought was readily available and in abundance. Various web sites confirmed what she had originally thought and all that she needed to do was turn a couple of everyday items into a murder weapon. June logged off from her laptop and set about finding what she required.

The bathroom in June's flat was compact to say the least but it housed a decent sized white washbasin mounted onto a vanity unit. Inside the unit cupboards she stored all her toiletries, often to excess.

Toothpastes, shampoos, shower gels and cans of hairspray, all bought when on special offers, filled both shelves to capacity. Tucked away behind her bargain stash was a roll of cotton wool sealed inside a plastic bag. That was the first thing she needed. June grabbed the bag, closed the cupboard door and set off to the kitchen.

In the bottom drawer of her kitchen units was a green fabric pouch with a red cross stamped on the top. This was June's first aid box that she had paid one pound for on one of her many bargain hunts. Taking it from the drawer for the first time since it had been purchased she hoped it would contain the other item she required. The Velcro fastening was hastily ripped apart and the contents emptied onto the worktop.

Just as she had suspected, the first aid kit contained a roll of crepe bandage, a sterile wipe, some gauze pieces and a roll of adhesive fabric tape. Everything needed to dress a wound in an emergency. The item that June was desperate to find was the sticky fabric tape. Now she had her tools, the next stage was to put them to good use.

The three unwanted items were squashed back into the container and returned to the kitchen drawer. She scooped up the cotton wool and tape and opened her cutlery drawer to grasp a pair of scissors. Within her hands she held what was to become a murder weapon.

The thought of being a murderer chilled June to the bone. Yet here she was about to construct something that she was to use to end a life. As she looked down at the items she was holding, her hands started to shake. Now her heart was racing and the pulsating sound in her ears was deafening. She had reached the point of no return and no matter how scared she was feeling, her life depended on what she was about to do. Her choice was a simple one. She had to take Denis Goodman's life or he would continue to ruin hers.

Sat at her dining table, June pulled out lumps of cotton wool and rolled them together to make a sausage shape. She soon had two tightly rolled sausages measuring just under an inch in diameter and about one and a half inches in length. The next stage was to wrap the tightly rolled cotton wool in fabric tape. The tape held all the bits of cotton wool together resembling two pellets. Her job was done, all

151

she had to do know was hold her nerve and wait for morning to come.

If there was a god, then she hoped he was still looking out for her and would give her the strength and opportunity to follow her plan through. Tomorrow Denis was going to die.

Chapter 37

June had not slept well, only managing to drift off for short spells. The enormity of what she was intending to do had dominated her thoughts and the churning in her abdomen had made it practically impossible to relax.

She could only manage a cup of coffee for her breakfast even though her stomach was telling her she needed food. Her anxiety level was sky high and she had already had three urgent trips to the toilet before taking her shower. She was taking short shallow breaths unable to maintain a normal rhythm, causing her to feel lightheaded. Panic had set in. This was going to be a Sunday she would remember for all time.

"Morning. I'll miss out the good. I'm still a bit fragile. What about you?" Maureen wasn't her usual cheery self as she met up with June.

"Hardly slept a wink and I'm starving but I couldn't swallow anything. I'll be glad when today is over," was June's honest reply.

"If you're implying by that last remark that something is going to happen today then please don't tell me what. If I know nothing then I can't say anything if I'm asked. Please, please be careful. I won't try and stop you but I can't condone what I suspect you have in mind." Maureen instinctively knew what her friend planned to do and wished it was otherwise.

Both women were tired and lacking any enthusiasm to chat about the usual mundane topics on their short walk to work. With each step she took, June's feet seemed to get heavier and heavier and her heart raced a little faster. Maureen had a sinking sensation in her stomach and a feeling of sheer dread spreading throughout her body.

As the handful of staff congregated for the morning meeting June caught sight of Denis being wheeled into the dining room for breakfast. Maureen had also spotted him. A knowing look passed between the friends. Both were making the same assumption, no serious damage had been done by June's vicious attack on him.

There had been no mention of any resident needing any special observation, which meant the prescription given must have eased Denis's bleeding. June was grateful for that. Whatever else was being mentioned in the meeting had gone over her head. She had only one thing on her mind and that was murder.

Breakfast was still being served in the dining room and a few of the slower diners were tucking into their scrambled egg, bacon and tomatoes. One old man sat alone at a table, clutching a fork with his left hand pushing around the contents of his plate. Before anyone else had the chance to go to his assistance, June made a beeline across the room to give him a helping hand.

"Good morning Denis love. Here, let me help you with your breakfast. Give me your fork, I'll cut it up or do you prefer a spoon?" she said in her faked caring manner.

On hearing her voice Denis looked up and for a split second their eyes met until he turned his head and looked away.

As she chopped up his food he remained silent, refusing to acknowledge her presence. Undeterred, June carried on expressing her false compassion speaking a little louder than normal for the benefit of those sat close by.

"Are you feeling better now Denis? You need to build your strength up sweetheart. You've been looking ever so fragile lately. Right, let's get some breakfast down you. Can you manage now?"

June put the cutlery down and he reached out for the fork in a determined effort to try and feed himself. June bent over so her face was close to his; almost touching his cheek. Very quietly she whispered in his ear, "Not long now, Denis. I'll be seeing you later."

Smiling, she turned and walked over to another couple of residents who were still eating and began chatting to them.

"Hello ladies. What have I missed while I've been off. What's the latest gossip then. You two know all what goes off in this place. You're a right pair of Hilda Ogden's."

The two women started grinning and nudging each other, delighted at the attention June was giving them. They were oblivious to the pained expression of their fellow diner, a condemned man who no longer had an appetite.

Sunday was always the most popular day of the week for visitors to Field Hall. A few came on Saturdays to see their elderly relatives but Sundays had always been the busiest day.

Family and friends would arrive throughout the day to spend a few hours with their loved ones. Or if the resident was up to it, they would often be taken from Field Hall for a day out. The building was usually a hive of activity and with so many strange faces floating in an out of residents rooms. June felt sure she could get Denis alone eventually.

Today, there would be no hiding place for Denis Goodman. After mauling his breakfast another member of staff had wheeled him into the day room and sat him amongst other residents. Some were watching television and a few were reading Sunday newspapers. Denis just stared at the television oblivious to his surroundings. The others sat around him ignoring the old man who had made no effort to communicate with them during the past few weeks. June was certain he would not be having any visitors as there were no other family members alive, except her.

The morning passed quickly with staff and visitors chatting about anything and everything. Many expressed their relief at knowing their elderly loved ones were being cared for by such friendly staff. June and Maureen had come to know many regular visitors over the years. Many felt they could confided in them regarding any concerns about their aging relative's status. Little did they know that one of those caring members of staff was planning to murder a resident.

At lunchtime Denis was yet again present in the dining room. It seemed obvious to two particular staff members that he was avoiding being alone. But, eventually he would have to return to his room and then his fate would be sealed.

June made her way to the dining room and once again offered to help Denis cut up his lunch which was roast pork and all the trimmings. Just as he had ignored her previously, he continued to avoid any eye contact while she stood close to him.

155

The dining room was only a quarter full as many had gone in to lunch at the earliest opportunity and wasted no time consuming their lunch. Many eagerly awaited a visit from their family members.

"Eat up Denis. You can have a nice long nap this afternoon," then June lowered the tone of her voice and whispered, "A very, very long nap."

She had decided that her tormenting was going to be relentless even though she was dreading what she was about to do.

Maureen stuck her head round the door and called her friend to come and have her lunch break, which the couple nearly always spent together. June bid Denis a fake, fond "see you later" and walked off to join her friend. The staff rest room was empty when the couple entered, so Maureen was able to speak freely.

"He's avoiding being in his room isn't he? Has he eaten anything today? My bloody nerves are jangling June and I'm not sure why. I will be glad to go home today and I hope you are with me when I do."

"Remember what you said this morning. What you don't know about you can't speak about. Don't ask me any more for your sake, please," June abruptly responded.

The tension was mounting between the friends. Maureen was beginning to question the old saying that ignorance is bliss. In this case she thought ignorance was bloody nerve racking. She had even offered up a few more silent prayers during the course of the morning, to any god that would listen.

Neither of the women had much of an appetite, ignoring their nervous rumbling stomachs. Coffee was all they managed to consume before returning to their work. The rest room clock was reading 1.00pm. June had only four hours to complete her macabre task if she was to carry out the threat she had been making.

The two women walked back through the reception area, both having a crafty glance towards the dining room. There was no wheelchair and no Denis to be seen, so June popped her head round the day room door. There was still no sign of him in there. The only other option was that he had returned to his room, possibly for a visit to the toilet.

Before she dare venture into room number five, June needed to be sure he was alone and that no one would see her sneaking in. She saw Sarah sat at the reception desk giving her full attention to the computer monitor.

Walking up the drive towards the front entrance June spotted a couple of regular visitors for one of their male residents. They were heading straight for reception. She immediately recognised the couple as Fred Hartley`s daughter and her husband who came to visit him every couple of weeks. This was possibly the opportunity June needed and instinctively put a hand in her tunic pocket. Her fingers touched the cotton wool pellets that were tucked neatly into a hankie in the corner of her pocket. She was armed with the tools she needed now she needed to keep her nerves steady. It was more than she could manage with her shaking hands.

"Hello. Are you both keeping well?" she asked the visitors as they opened the front door and walked towards her, trying to stop her voice from faltering. Both smiled at her and reassured her they were well. She now had an alibi, if needed. She was chatting in reception around the time of Denis`s demise.

Sarah was busy getting Fred`s family to sign the visitors book in keeping with fire regulations, to pay too much attention to June moving swiftly away.

With every step June made towards Denis`s room her legs felt heavier and heavier. Her heart was racing so fast she could hardly draw breath. As she reached the end of the corridor she stopped and turned to face the door of number five. She knocked gently and placed her shaking right hand on the door handle turning it slightly. A gentle push of the door and it opened allowing her to peer round it.

Her eyes immediately met his. He was sat in the armchair watching television as if he was waiting for her to come to him. She could taste bile rising in the back of her throat as a wave of nausea swept over her. Her entire body was shaking as she closed the door behind her. He turned his head to the left and faced the wall not making a sound.

June walked slowly towards him, her legs feeling so weak they felt as if they could collapse from under her at any second. He just continued to look away. His left hand was clutching the television remote pad close to his chest. A very frail old man who could offer her no resistance sat before her.

Adrenalin was pumping through June's body so fast it made her feel as if she was having an out of body experience. She sat on the chair arm looking at him, so old and helpless. A shell of the man she hated so much. Words came pouring from her mouth.

"I hate you Denis. I hate what you did to me and what you've made me into. Why did you come back? Why? I can't let you ruin my life again. You must understand that. I have to do this. May God forgive me."

Tears were streamed down her cheeks as her right hand reached into her pocket and felt for the homemade pellets. Her other hand pulled a cotton handkerchief from the pocket. "God forgive me," she whispered again. Her left hand holding the handkerchief grabbed Denis by his jaw, pulling his face towards her.

Using all the strength her shaking hand could muster she forced his mouth firmly shut. He still avoided looking her in the eyes.

Holding a pellet between her right forefinger and thumb she pushed it up his left nostril, as far as possible. Within seconds the other nostril had been blocked by a second pellet. His airways were all sealed off and Denis started to struggle for breath.

Thrashing his head from side to side made no difference to June's firm grip on his jaw. His left arm was trapped between June's body and the armchair back. With what little strength he had left in his legs, Denis tried to kick out but to no avail.

She saw the colour of his face change from grey to a reddish blue and for a split second she thought of releasing her grip. Then he made eye contact with her.

The eyes staring so fiercely into hers were not those of a defenceless old man. She saw the haunting, chilling eyes of her abuser; her rapist. The eyes that she had feared for so many years made her shudder.

The hate that June had suppressed for so long was now rising up inside her as she held his face even tighter.

"God will forgive me but he will never forgive you Denis. You're going to hell!"

As she spoke his body stopped struggling. Looking into his dying eyes she spoke her last words to him.

"Remember this is our little secret."

His once evil, deep brown eyes were now without any sign of life. The windows to his soul had closed.

If he wasn't dead he was only seconds from it. June could not stop and reflect on what she had done. She had to get out of his room and leave no trace of her malicious act.

Firstly, she pulled out the two cotton wool pellets from his nostrils and removed her other hand from his jaw. The cotton hankie would stop any obvious finger or thumb prints. She had read about it in a recent best-selling novel. The evidence was stuffed back in her pocket.

Denis had lost his grip on the television remote pad but it was still on his lap. His head had slumped forward as if he had nodded off to sleep. There was no reason for her to touch him again. June looked up at the television screen, she didn't need to turn it off. Hopefully it would look like Denis had slipped peacefully away watching the 1.00pm news when they came to estimate his time of death.

She needed to get out of the room and fast, but not before she had wiped away the wet patches on her cheeks and mopped up any teardrops that were clinging to her eyelashes. The hankie that had held Denis's mouth shut was now mopping up his murderer's tears.

She had no idea how long she'd been in the room but knew she had to get back and circulate amongst the staff and residents immediately to allay any suspicions.

Closing the door as quietly as she could and checking there was no one busy bodying in the corridor, June inhaled deeply and walked back towards reception. She had walked up the corridor as a caring member of staff but returned as a cold blooded murderer. That sickening thought repulsed her. Her mouth felt suddenly very dry and her stomach queasy. *What have I just done?*

Sarah was still engrossed with whatever she was doing on the computer as June made her entrance back into the reception area.

Another couple of visitors were just opening the front door and everyone exchanged smiles. June was praying no one would notice the little blotches on her face that her salty tears had left behind or her pallor from the nausea she was feeling.

If she couldn't get to a toilet pretty damn quick she would end up spewing her guts up on the spot. She briskly crossed the path of the two visitors managing to just mumble, "Hello again" and dash off to the staff loos.

Sinking to her knees, she flung her arms around the toilet pan and began to retch. Having missed eating lunch all that came up was a small amount of bile and copious amounts of saliva. Dizziness was making her start to sweat profusely. The horrendous reality of what she had just done was hitting home.

The words "Forgive me God, please forgive me," were followed by another bout of fruitless retching.

Maureen had noticed June was nowhere to be seen and was starting to panic. Whatever she was up to she instinctively knew it was not going to be anything good. The expression, worried sick, just about explained the way Maureen was feeling at that moment. Her sixth sense was telling her that June was with Denis and no way was she going into his room to find her friend. Whatever was going on behind that closed door, she dare not even try and imagine.

After what seemed like an eternity of waiting, Maureen finally caught sight of June coming towards her in the reception area. It was obvious that she was returning from the staff rest room or toilet section situated up a narrow hallway behind Reception. Just one look at June's face told Maureen her suspicions were correct. Trouble was in the air.

"Where the fuck have you been? No! Don't tell me, I can fucking guess!" Maureen's voice was full of nervous anger and she had felt the need to express her rage by the use of certain crude expletives.

"Am I not allowed to go to the loo now?" was the surly reply from her very nervy friend.

"Loo, my arse! I have been shitting bricks wondering what you were up to." Maureen's language was becoming more colourful as she vented her anger.

"I'm here now so what's to be done?" was all the explanation June was prepared to give as she stormed off towards the day room with a furious friend marching behind her.

A handful of residents were watching television in the comfort of their high seated chairs. Some had already had visitors and were settling down for a relaxing afternoon. Others were simply there for the company because they were not expecting anyone to call.

June took it upon herself to cheer everyone up before it was time for afternoon tea and biscuits. She just needed to keep active and totally occupied, hoping her bouts of vomiting had passed. Her nausea had been replaced by a numbness of mind and body blocking out all thoughts of what she had just done.

The serenity of the Sabbath at Field Hall was totally disrupted and turned into Bedlam with just three words.

"Call an ambulance!"

On hearing the distress call echoing down the corridor both June and Maureen froze on the spot throwing panicking glances at each other.

The sight of nurse Sarah Stead running towards the end of the first corridor which housed Denis Goodman's room was the two women's worst nightmares. For Maureen it was the moment she had been dreading ever since the day her friend had confided in her. For June it was a reality check on the crime she had committed.

Sandra Yates had been taking the tea trolley to the resident's rooms. Hot drinks and biscuits were offered to visitors who were spending time alone with their nearest and dearest. Sandra had gone to offer the resident of room number five a cup of tea and found him slumped in his armchair. Fearing the worst, Sandra had asked for an ambulance to be called.

Sarah, the registered nurse had rushed to Denis's room while calling 999 on her mobile phone.

What had Sandra discovered? That was foremost in Maureen's mind.

June knew what the panic was about but was praying it looked as if an old man had been struck down by a fatal stroke or a massive heart attack. As sure as hell there would be a post mortem and the following days were going to be long and anxious for her. Her entire future now depended on the outcome.

An ambulance arrived within minutes preceded by a young male paramedic carrying a resuscitation kit. Not knowing what was happening behind the door of number five was agonising for the two friends until the door finally opened.

Sarah and Sandra were the first to come out of Denis's room followed by the paramedic. Finally the ambulance crew emerged and the two women's last sighting of Denis Goodman was of him strapped onto a stretcher and being carried out to the waiting ambulance.

What June observed as she glanced at the body on the stretcher knocked her for six. Denis had an oxygen mask strapped to his face. He wasn't dead.

What had started out as a normal Sunday at Field Hall had descended into one of panic and total confusion. Everyone was asking about Denis's sudden ill health and how it had come about. Conversations between staff and residents had taken place which were supposed to calm the tense atmosphere but they hadn't done so. What had happened to him? Had he shown any signs of not feeling well? Did he have any family that should be informed? These were just a few of the constant stream of questioning the staff members were asking and being asked.

Maureen's head was in a spin with all the goings on. Not wanting to know the truth about Denis's condition and how it came about but overcome with curiosity to know if June had been the root cause was nerve racking.

June was in turmoil with the feeling of relief that she may not have murdered another human. Yet she feared that if he survived, the truth may come to light. Again Denis Goodman had thrown her into another living nightmare.

162

Mrs. McLellan, the manager, had been doing her bit to calm the other residents, reassuring them that Denis was in good hands and would be receiving the best possible care. Any news on his progress would be relayed to everyone and the hospital had assured her they would call with regular updates.

When it came to the end of their shift and no update on Denis's progress had been received, Maureen and June walked home in silence. One of them was too afraid to ask and the other too afraid to reveal what had happened behind the door of number five.

Chapter 38

Two women spent an agonising sleepless night, both tormented by the unknown.

After arriving home, June had suffered another bout of dizziness and vomiting made worse by not having eaten. The thought of being a cold blooded murderer had really upset her. If Denis survived, then even if he could not spill the beans to anyone she would have no choice than to resign. It would be impossible for her to carry on working at Field Hall, facing him every day, never been able to forget what a vile act she had committed.

Confessing all to her friend had given her so much comfort at the time and the close bond the pair had formed had meant so much to June. Now she was probably going to lose Maureen`s friendship. Whatever the outcome of the horrendous situation, Denis Goodman was going to be the cause of her heartache and loss once again.

Maureen Jones had gone home from work not knowing what to think anymore. She spent a sleepless night trying to imagine what her friend had endured as a child, both physically and emotionally, at the hands of an evil paedophile. *Did it justify the acts of revenge that had been inflicted upon him? Should she clear her conscience and report all she knew to Mrs. McLellan? If she did and Denis died would that make her an accomplice?*

Deprived of sleep from the endless questions Maureen had asked herself and disturbing images that she had conjured up in her mind, she was exhausted when her alarm clock started to beep. Her stomach was growling, begging for food but she had no appetite.

She managed to force a slice of toast and a cup of coffee down her throat after a hot shower. But even the hot water couldn`t take away the cold and numbness she was feeling. Her whole body seemed to be overpowered with a feeling of doom, dreading what news was awaiting her when she arrived at work.

Both women were too tired to even bother speaking to each other as they met up for their walk to work. An air of despondency had taken over from which there seemed no escape.

The only real sign of any communication between the two women when they arrived at Field Hall on that cold and frosty morning was eye contact. As they hung up their coats and scarves and locked up their bags, Maureen and June looked at each other and were able to read each other's thoughts. What had happened to Denis? Was he dead or alive? Neither woman knew which would be the better outcome.

As the day shift staff members assembled for their morning briefing June started to feel sick again. She had only managed a cup of coffee for breakfast and like her friend, her stomach was desperate for food. Her legs had started to tremble slightly and to keep her hands from shaking she had to grip them tightly together, praying no one noticed. Both women had done an awful lot of praying in the past few days. Would their prayers be answered?

Jean Hartley, the night shift nurse, started to speak about the events of the previous night. Nothing unusual had happened. It had been a peaceful night in stark contrast to the chaotic Sunday afternoon. Then her tone of voice changed and she spoke in a more sombre mood.

"I'm sorry to say that Denis Goodman passed away at 6.35 pm last night. We are not sure exactly what was the cause of death is but I expect there will a post mortem. He was alive when the paramedics arrived. He had a very faint pulse and I believe the emergency team did resuscitate him here, but he went into cardiac arrest at the hospital and there was no more they could do. For now that is all I know but I'm sure Mrs. McLellan will keep us informed when we get more information."

Denis Goodman had not made himself very popular during his short stay at Field Hall with either staff or fellow residents, so any sadness on his passing was not on the same scale as that felt for Ivy Grimshaw.

Maureen Jones felt very sad at his passing but not because she would miss Denis in the slightest. His demise was caused by her friend, of that she was almost certain. She felt sure the proverbial shit was going to hit a bloody big fan and when that shit finally came to rest it would be on her friend's head. *Would some of that shit also land on her?* That was another very worrying thought that was buzzing around in her frantic thoughts.

June nearly had her own cardiac arrest when she heard the news about Denis. As much as she had wanted him out of her life, the confirmation that she had killed him disgusted her. Even as he lay on a gurney at the local mortuary he was still able to cause her heartache. *Would he still cause her grief from beyond his grave? Now that she had carried out her threats and got rid of him, was it really worth all the stress and anxiety she was now feeling?* Questions, questions, questions, so many she had asked herself and many more to answer.

Chapter 39

Wednesday 28th March 2012

Two days had passed since the announcement of Denis Goodman's sudden death. After hearing the news on Monday, the two friends had barely spoken to each other and that had only been to discuss important work issues.

Neither woman wanted to discuss Denis's passing but both were desperate to hear the outcome of his post mortem. The past couple of days had seen both Maureen and June functioning on auto pilot, just going through their daily work routine like robots. One or two residents had noticed their lack of enthusiasm and asked what troubled them. A common virus seemed to be accepted as a good enough excuse by everyone.

It was just gone 3.00 pm on Wednesday afternoon when the phone call from the Coroner's office came through. Mrs. McLellan had taken the call and made her way through to the reception area to inform Nurse Sarah Stead of the verdict.

Maureen was the next staff member to get the news. She had been passing through to the day room when Sarah had called her over. Within seconds of hearing the verdict, Maureen scuttled off to find June, who was pouring cups of tea in the dining room. At her first opportunity she made her excuses to join her friend to disclose the dreaded news.

The two women finally managed to get a few minutes alone in the staff room while taking their break. Maureen couldn't wait to blurt out the news.

"The Coroner's verdict is natural causes. It seems Denis suffered atrial fibrillation and that makes his heartbeat go funny and with having had one stroke it had probably caused him to have another stroke as well. I think I've got that right. Sarah was using all these fancy medical words but I think I got the gist of it. I didn't like to ask too much or appear too interested. Anyway it was natural causes. I thought you'd want to know."

"Thank you. Thank you," was all June could manage to say.

"Do you want to talk about it? I can stop off at yours later if you want. Have a think about it."

Maureen didn't want to push her friend but now they had the verdict her curiosity was getting the better of her. Just knowing there was not going to be any shit hitting any fan had lightened her mood. Would it improve her friend's?

At the end of their shift the two women were putting on their coats and opening their lockers when June finally responded to her friend's question.

"If you've got time I can put the kettle on and open a packet of Jaffa cakes."

"McVities or Morrison's own?" Maureen was trying to lighten the atmosphere.

"Don't push it!" was June's sharp reply but for the first time in days she had a faint smile on her face.

Chapter 40

"You can't beat a Jaffa cake and a cup of tea. How many calories in one biscuit? I forget. But I know it's not a lot," Maureen mumbled whilst dunking another biscuit in her cup of tea. She was trying to get a conversation started without touching on the real reason for the two women being sat on June's sofa.

"I neither know nor care anymore. After the last few days I must have lost a couple of stones." June was steering their chat towards Denis Goodman's sudden death.

"Do you want to know exactly what happened to him or not? Once I spill the beans there's no going back. You'll probably wish you'd never asked."

Maureen took a large mouthful of tea, closed her eyes and gave out a big sigh before replying.

"I think I'm in it up to my neck anyway. I knew the frame of mind you were in and I knew you were going to do something to him. So, whatever happened on Sunday I probably could have stopped it. I think that makes me an accomplice in the eyes of the law."

"I could be sick now just thinking about what I did but here goes..."

June drew in a long deep breath and started to recall the murderous assault she had made on Denis, not holding back any of the unsavoury details. As she reached the part where Denis had started to struggle, tears flooded her eyes and her voice started to falter. She managed to finish her gruesome tale then sank back into the comfort of her sofa as her shoulders started to heave. Tears began to flow like a mountain stream rolling down her cheeks and off her chin like raindrops.

Maureen remained silent. Sitting perfectly still she digested what she had just heard.

"I think I'd be speechless if I'd just heard my friend was a murderer. I suffocated an old man who couldn't put up any resistance. I'm an evil bitch and I've stooped to his level. How do I live with that?" June paused to wipe away tears from her face and wiped the dew drops hanging from her nose with a tissue pulled from her pocket. Then she continued, "I should have stopped, I thought about it when I saw him struggling."

Maureen finally broke her silence and in a calm and gentle manner asked a question.

"You said that when he started to struggle you hesitated and was about to stop. So what was it that made you carry on? Something happened to tip the scales because I know you. You could never have stood there and watched him die."

June closed her eyes before she continued, "Every time I close my eyes I can see him shaking his head, panicking and I feel sick. His eyes were starting to bulge and I could see the colour of his face changing and then...and then...his eyes...his eyes changed. He looked into my eyes and ...I saw him! It wasn't the old man looking at me anymore it was my leering uncle staring at me just like he did when he was touching me...raping me ..."

"So, it wasn't a frail and helpless old man you were angry at, it was your rapist, your abuser, who you wanted to hurt. I can understand that. You didn't finish him off anyway. Maybe you subconsciously knew he'd only passed out when you left him. If you had wanted to make sure he was well and truly dead you would have checked before you left his room." Maureen's calm explanation was not damning or condescending. Then she continued, "He's finally out of your life, so now's your chance to make a fresh start. Put him and all the crap you've been carrying around behind you now. That evil piece of shit isn't worth a second thought anyway. There's some others out there who he abused who will never know what became of him. Let's hope he's gone straight to hell. Better still, let's go to his bloody funeral and make sure they burn the bastard."

June had tears in her eyes again as she listened to Maureen's interpretation of events. She realised her friend was not apportioning blame and was still offering her support. Most importantly she had

170

not lost her friendship. Denis had failed to destroy the most important thing that June had in her life. All anxiety she had been bottling up was finally started to melt away with every tear she was shedding.

Maureen said very little after suggesting they go to his funeral. She was content just to sit beside her tearful friend and wait for June to rid herself of guilt. With every sob and tear that fell a little bit more faded away.

***

Denis Goodman's funeral was held at Burtley crematorium at 11.00am Monday 2nd April. It was the simplest of affairs with no relatives in attendance. The only two mourners sat in the tiny chapel were Maureen Jones and June Cowburn who were representing the staff and residents of Field Hall Care Home.

The two women had been seated in the back pew, listening to some clergyman spouting about Denis being welcomed into Heaven and having gone to a better place. The poor chap had obviously no idea what or who he was talking about.

The two bogus mourners sat at the back had their own ideas about where Denis was heading for all eternity and it wasn't God's Heaven.

When the crimson velvet curtain was finally drawn, obscuring the pine coffin with just one single wreath laid upon it, the two mourners looked at each other, smiled and simultaneously whispered. "Good riddance."

Both women were convinced that was the last they would ever see or hear about the evil Denis Goodman.

Chapter 41

Wednesday June 26th 2012

Three months had passed since the death of Denis Goodman. He had long been forgotten by his fellow residents and staff at Field Hall, except for two women who were the only ones to know the real reason for his sudden passing.

June Cowburn had slowly returned to living a normal life again and had regained her bubbly, friendly personality. Maureen Jones had got her old friend back and the two women were planning on taking a holiday together. Everything was looking good for their futures.

June had walked home from work with her friend as usual that day. They had chatted away about everything and anything that had happened during their shift. Both were looking forward to taking a relaxing bath and a night in front of their television sets. As they reached the entrance to June's flat, they said their farewells and Maureen carried on walking the short distance to her house.

Inside the communal hallway June checked on her mail box and picked up a pile of junk mail that had been deposited for her.

She'd sifted through the handful of flyers and charity bags finding nothing of any interest until she pulled out a long white envelope tucked between them. It was addressed to her personally and marked "If undelivered please return to" on the back. It was a very official looking letter and obviously not a demand for payment.

With her door closed behind her and the safety chain engaged, June dropped her bag and ripped open the white envelope.

The letter was on quality paper which was obvious by the feel of it. The embossed letter heading was in red and black spelling out Hawkin, Hawkin & Dawson solicitors of Brownhill Road, Burtley.

Intrigued, she read the letter slowly. It was short and to the point. The letter asked June to contact the solicitor's office and make an appointment at her earliest convenience. It's content left her confused and very curious. She felt totally clueless as to what it could be about. It could wait until the next day she'd decided. The letter was returned to the envelope and put into June's handbag for safe keeping.

After a long soak and a microwaved ready meal, curiosity got the better of June and she fished the mysterious letter out of her handbag. She could think of no reason why a solicitor would want to contact her, unless it was the written equivalent of telephone cold calling. Convinced that if she rang the number on the letter it would be someone on the other end of the line suggesting she made a will and probably an offer to help her write one for a substantial fee. She put the letter back in her bag.

After a night's viewing of Emmerdale, Eastenders and an episode of her favourite murder mystery programme, June called it a day and turned off her television. She turned off all her lamps, lights and electrical gadgets, paid a last visit to the toilet then settled down in her bed.

As she pulled the duvet up to her neck and rolled onto her side she had one last thought about the letter she had received. *Perhaps she should ring the solicitors and make sure it was just another way of touting for business. If it was she would give them a piece of her mind in no uncertain terms.* Decision made, she closed her eyes and waited for sleep to come.

Chapter 42

June had been in bed for almost nine hours and awoke feeling relaxed and refreshed. With two days off, she had decided to spend a few hours out shopping for some holiday clothes and to get some brochures from the local travel agent.

Maureen was favouring a week in Benidorm after watching the television comedy series. June was feeling giddy at just the thought of a week in the Spanish sun. It was 8.30 am and with an exciting day ahead of her, June sprang out of bed and headed straight for the bathroom. Within ten minutes she was showered and wrapped up in her old bathrobe. Another ten minutes passed and she had dried her hair and was ready for the day.

With her appetite fully restored another cooked breakfast was quickly wolfed down with a mug of tea. As she drained the last sip of tea from the mug, she remembered the letter in her handbag. She decided she would ring the solicitors and find out just what all the urgency was about.

"Hawkins, Hawkins and Dawson solicitors, Lisa speaking."

"Good morning Lisa, My name`s Mrs. June Cowburn and I`ve received a letter asking me to contact your office. Can you tell me what it`s all about please?"

"Good morning Mrs. Cowburn. Can you tell me the reference on the top left hand side of your letter please."

"RDH/LH240612."

"Okay. Right, Mrs. Cowburn the letter is from Richard Hawkin one of our solicitors. He would like you to make an appointment to come along and see him."

"This isn`t some time wasting attempt to get me to your office is it? And when I get there he`ll try and talk me into writing a will or something."

"No way, Mrs. Cowburn. Whatever Mr. Hawkin wishes to speak to you about it is certainly nothing like that. Can I make you an appointment?"

"Can you fit me in today, I have the day off and I'll be in your area later on? Believe me it had better not be some wild goose chase!"

"Believe me Mrs. Coburn. It`s all above board. Can you come in for 1.45 pm?"

"1.45 pm. Okay."

"Fine. We`ll see you this afternoon. Thank you for calling."

Chapter 43

Hawkin, Hawkin & Dawson had been based in Burtley for as long as June could remember. She had used another company to represent her when Nigel had filed for divorce. That had been the only time she had ever needed to hire the services of a solicitor.

The small waiting room was more clinical than she imagined it would be with just a few chairs and a selection of posh magazines on a shelf. The plain magnolia walls had posters advertising a variety of services ranging from family counselling sessions to accident compensation. *All nice little money spinners*, June thought.

She didn`t have to wait long before a tall, slim middle aged man entered the waiting room and ushered her across the hall into a typical solicitor`s office. He was a stereotype solicitor dressed in a blue two piece pin striped suit with white shirt and plain blue tie. June guessed his age at around fifty because his dark hair was speckled with grey. He was still an attractive looking chap.

"Good afternoon, I`m Richard Hawkins. Please come through to my office and take a seat Mrs. Cowburn. Now you must be wondering why we needed to contact you."

"I certainly am and it had better not be to waste my time."

"No, no, rest assured it`s nothing like that. Would you like a cup of tea or coffee before we start?"

"No thank you. Please just tell me why I`m here."

"Right. We`ll crack on then. Mrs. Cowburn, we have been trying to trace you for a few weeks now. Could you confirm your date of birth and your maiden name, please."

"Why? What have I supposed to have done for God`s sake?"

"Please, I need to confirm who you are."

"Twenty six, six, nineteen sixty, Sweet. Okay?"

"Fine. Now I am the executor for the estate of Denis Arnold Goodman, who I believe was your uncle. Did you know he had passed away?"

June couldn't comprehend what was being said.

"Can I take it this has all come as a surprise to you Mrs. Cowburn?"

"Errr...yes."

"Well he died in March. He wasn't a wealthy man, far from it but he did make a will, way back in 1970. That will has never been replaced or altered so it still stands today. You are his named recipient and closest surviving relative so his estate passes to you."

"Err... What exactly does that mean? This is a real shock."

"Well, there was money in a bank account. From that we had to pay for his funeral costs and a few sundry items. Our fee comes out of that as well. Whatever is left over goes to you. But, like I said earlier it's not a grand amount."

"How much exactly?"

"This cheque is made out to you for £1,306.39."

"Right. You say I am the only surviving relative."

"Correct. We traced you from records which confirmed you had married and changed your name."

"Thank you."

"My pleasure Mrs. Cowburn. Now, there was one other thing. When his personal belongings were collected from Field Hall Care Home, which was his last place of residence, there was an envelope. The envelope was addressed to our company with an instruction that it must be handed to us in the event of his death. Inside the envelope was another sealed envelope. This one was addressed to...June Sweet, your maiden name, which I am now passing on to you. There are a few more small personal items in a bag as well. Nothing much. Just a signet ring, a watch and some old photographs. Like I say, there's not a lot but it is all yours now. You seem very shocked Mrs. Cowburn. Are you sure I can't get you a cup of tea or a glass of water even?"

"Yes, a glass of water would be nice, thank you."

Ten minutes later, with the envelope, cheque and a jiffy bag tucked into her handbag June left Hawkin, Hawkin & Dawson's premises. Any plans that she had made for the rest of her day were forgotten. The only thing on her mind once again was Denis Arnold Goodman.

How June had managed not to faint when the solicitor handed over the envelope to her she would never know. How she had managed to walk back home after leaving the solicitors offices was another mystery. The second Denis`s name was mentioned everything had become surreal.

There was the suave Mr. Hawkin thinking he was conveying good news when he was actually delivering one almighty body blow that threw her mind into turmoil all over again.

Instead of calling into the travel agents as she had originally planned, June had made her way straight back home. Her hands were shaking so badly it took her three attempts to put her door key into the lock. Once inside she made straight for the lounge and opened the sideboard door, feeling for a small bottle of brandy that was in there. Not bothering to use a glass, she unscrewed the cap and downed a large mouthful straight from the bottle. Once the warmth of the liquid reached her stomach she replaced the cap and put the brandy back in the sideboard. Another mouthful would have been better but June knew she needed to try and clear her head.

Sitting on her sofa with the faded, slightly dog eared envelope in her hand she stared at the handwriting. It was addressed to June Sweet. But she had been Cowburn for well over a decade. So she surmised the letter must have been written a long time ago. Denis had obviously not known that his niece had married.

June just stared at the two words concentrating on the handwriting. There was only one way to find out what was in the envelope and that was to open it. *And once I have opened it will I wish I hadn`t?* Again, even from the depths of hell, where she hoped he had gone, Denis was able to play with her mind.

Then her thoughts turned to the cheque she had just been given. No way was she ever going to accept any money from him either. That was easy to deal with. She could just tear the cheque up or burn it.

The tot of brandy had been enough to have a calming effect. Her rapid heartbeat had slowed and her shaking hands had become a little steadier. June braced herself to tear open the envelope.

A sheet of neatly folded A4 paper was all that the envelope contained. June unfolded the paper to reveal more of Denis's handwriting and began to read.

14th February 1972

My Dearest June,

Please forgive me for leaving you so suddenly. You must believe me when I say I had no choice than to move out of the area.

I know I must have broken your young heart and I am truly sorry but you must believe me when I say I love you. You were and always will be my special little girl. What we shared together was so beautiful and I will treasure the memories of our special times together. You will be forever in my heart.

My love always
Denis xx

"Maureen, can you come over? I need you to see something. I can't explain on the phone but....he's back!"

"Who's back? Calm down June. Who's back?"

"Denis! He's...he's playing with my head again. Please, I need you to see something." June's disturbing plea had her friend worried.

"I'm in town, shopping, but I can get over in about ten minutes. Calm down and make yourself a cup of tea. Do you hear me June? I'm on my way over."

"Thanks. Thank you."

Still shaking from the shock of what she had just read, June put down her mobile phone and tried to slow down her palpitations by taking deep breaths. Relaxing slightly, she slumped back into the sofa and rested her head against the soft leather. Beside her on the cushion lay the note, screwed into a ball in a fit of anger. She didn't want to look at Denis's handwriting and sick sentiments again.

179

As promised, Maureen arrived a little over ten minutes later, slightly breathless due to having carried a heavy shopping bag the length of Burtley` High street.

"What`s all this about Denis then? How do you mean he`s back. He`s bloody dead, we both know that," she said struggling to take off her shoes at the entrance hall of June`s flat. "I thought you`d got over all that crap and moved on," she continued.

"So did I until today. The bastard has only left a will and guess who`s his only sodding living relative?" June`s anxiety was turning to anger now she had her rock, her friend.

"A will! I thought he had nowt. He`d been in prison for fucks sake. Don`t tell me he was worth a fucking fortune as well." Maureen was confused and irritated.

June waited until both were sat on the sofa then started to explain about the solicitor`s letter arriving. As she got closer to telling her friend about the estate she had inherited she was almost garbling.

"Slow down. So you got a letter to see a solicitor and it was about Denis. Have I got this right? Has he left some cash in his will and it goes to you?"

"Not just cash. There`s a letter for me that he wrote after he scarpered. It`s sick, he was sick."

"June, he is not here anymore. He was sick but he`s gone. Where`s this letter then?" Maureen was now very curious about the letter.

The screwed up paper was firmly clutched in June`s hand but she dropped it onto Maureen`s lap. Trying to straighten out the creases wasn`t easy but she managed to flatten the paper sufficiently enough to make the writing readable.

Maureen scrutinised every word and when she reached the end slowly laid the paper on her lap. She remained silent for few seconds then started to speak quietly.

"He was one sick bastard. Not only sick, he was deluded. How could he possibly think you had feelings for him when he was...."

"Raping me!" June said the words her friend had hesitated to say.

"Was this all he left you?"

"No. There's a cheque for... I can't remember how much but I won't be cashing it. Oh, there's a bag with some stuff in...personal stuff. But I've not opened it yet. It's in my handbag. I'll get it. I don't want to open it on my own."

June walked over to the dining table, opened up her handbag and pulled up a brown jiffy bag. She passed it to Maureen and sat back down beside her.

"You open it for me. I don't want to touch anything that belonged to him. I think the solicitor said there's a ring and his watch. Open it for me, please," June was pleading with her friend.

"I'm not so keen on handling his stuff either. Sick bastard! But, here goes."

Maureen tore open the adhesive flap, and turned the bag upside down. The contents spilled out onto her legs that were covered by dark blue denim jeans.

Both women stared in silence at what they saw on Maureen's lap. As expected there was an old wristwatch with a tatty brown leather strap, a man's gold signet ring and a pile of old dog eared photographs. What came as a complete shock to both women was something that was just visible between the photos... a bottle green satin ribbon.

"That's one of my hair ribbons. I wore those for junior school when my hair was long. How did he...no why did he want one of my ribbons? He's kept it all these years. How sick is that?"

"God only knows what went on in his head. Let's have a look at these photos. I hope there's nothing disgusting in this lot."

Maureen started to turn the photos face upwards. The images were all of little girls. As she turned over another picture June snatched up a handful.

"It's me. The photos are all of me!"

Maureen took the photos out of June's hand and gathered all the images together in her hands. She knelt down on the beige carpet and started to lay out the photos in a row. With every one that was placed on the carpet it became obvious that all the images were of the same little girl. That little girl was obviously June.

Fourteen photographs were laid out on the carpet. Each picture was of June at various stages in her childhood. Some were of her as a baby, but the others were more disturbing images of her. One was in a swimsuit at the seaside and one of her as a toddler in just a pair of shorts playing in a garden. There was one that had been taken of a little girl standing up naked in a bath. The child was no more than two years old and it was without any doubt the same child as all the other images. Denis had kept a collection of photographs of June throughout her childhood.

"So, he kept all these pictures of you but none of anyone or anything else. Now that is disturbing. He really was obsessed with his own niece. Did he ever have a girlfriend, boyfriend even?" Maureen asked with real concern in her voice.

"I can`t remember seeing him with anybody. He was always round at our house. I think my mum just thought he was a bit lonely so he came round to ours a lot. But after seeing all this and that bloody letter, it looks as if it was me he wanted to be near. I feel sick at the thought of him ogling me as a child."

Shocked by what lay in front of them and the realisation of just how perverted Denis Goodman had really been, the women sat speechless for a few minutes. June was the one to air her concerns first.

"I`m going to burn the bloody cheque. I don`t want anything to do with his estate. Estate, that`s a bloody laugh in itself. We both assumed he had been cremated with the compliments of the state. Obviously not!"

"Look, it`s entirely your decision and I can go along with you not wanting anything that belonged to him, but it`s a lot of money that could be put to good use." Maureen was trying to think more rationally than her distressed friend. She continued, "How about this for an option...send the money to a charity. Pick a charity you would like to help. And, there`s a pawn shop in town that will cash cheques for a bit of a fee so the cheque you have won`t have to be paid into your account first. I think the shop is buying gold as well so you could weigh in his ring for a bit more cash."

June sat for a few minutes pondering over Maureen's suggestions, then answered.

"Childline. Yes, Childline can have the cash. It's an appropriate choice. It may just help one child to avoid going through the crap I've been through."

"Brilliant choice! Now get that laptop booted up and we can find out where to send the cash to. There's no time like the present as our mum used to say. So, pull yourself together girl, get some slap on and let's be charitable with the bastard's money." Maureen was on a mission to get her friend back on track and eradicate Denis Goodman from their lives for ever again.

"What about the photographs? I don't want them either. I'll burn them." June was getting some of her strength and determination back. "No, be a mate and burn them for me. The thought that he might have been ogling them makes me sick and heaven knows what else he may have been doing when he's had them in his clammy mitts. Burn that bloody ribbon as well!"

"Consider it done chuck!"

Chapter 44

Denis`s signet ring and watch had been sold for scrap value and added to the amount June had managed to get from the cashing of the solicitor`s cheque. Childline would be getting an anonymous donation of over £1,300.

Knowing that the cash may just help a child escape from the clutches of a brutal or abusing adult gave June great pleasure. The irony of a sexual predator's money being used in such a way was very satisfying.

The wad of cash had been sealed into a white jiffy bag and was propped up on June`s sideboard just ready to post. She had arranged to meet Maureen at lunchtime in the High street and their plan was to send the jiffy bag anonymously by Special delivery. Both women were hoping that when the packet was handed over the Post Office counter it would be the very last time they would ever have to think of Denis Goodman. They had planned to celebrate by booking their holiday.

As punctual as she always was, Maureen was waiting outside the Post Office looking very casual dressed in white cropped trousers and a loose fitting pale yellow blouse with a pair of sun glasses perched on her nose. On seeing her friend June immediately commented on her friend`s attire.

"You look as if you`re ready to get on the plane and we`ve not booked the holiday yet."

"After the last few months it can`t come soon enough for me. Let`s kiss that flaming money goodbye and get our arses into the travel agents. Benidorm here we come!" Maureen was bubbling with excitement.

The queue in the Post Office snaked up and down the length of the building twice. Being lunchtime, only half of the cashier`s windows were in use. The two women patiently shuffled along, slowly getting nearer to the front of the queue. Eventually, they made it to the front and were waiting for the flashing sign to tell them which window to go to.

"Bloody hell, I've had shorter pregnancies than the time it's taken us to get here!" Maureen was fed up of waiting and eager to get her holiday sorted.

"Shhhh. We're nearly there. We won't be long now," June whispered, hoping no one heard her friend's last sarcastic remark.

Within minutes the jiffy bag had become the property of Royal Mail and the women bid good riddance to Denis Goodman and all he stood for. Next stop was the travel agents.

Finally, Maureen had persuaded her friend that Benidorm was the perfect destination for their holiday and the booking had been confirmed and paid for. In the last week of July the Costa Blanca would be playing host to Birtley's answer to Thelma and Louise.

"Oh this year we're off to sunny Spain, ye viva Espana," Maureen had started to sing with giddy excitement as they left the travel shop.

"We're not going to the Costa Brava you dipstick. It's Blanca not Brava," June pointed out her friend's mistake.

"Same difference! I don't give a toss as long as I get a week full of sun, sea, sand and sex."

"Sex! Did you just say sex?"

"If I'm lucky. It's been a long time since I had a man. I'm not going to turn down the chance of a shaaaa..." The frown on June's face stopped Maureen from completing her sentence but she continued, "Alright, I get the message but I can dream can't I? I'll be packing my best thongs just on the off chance."

The thought of seeing Maureen wearing a thong had June smiling as she asked, "What next? Do you fancy a coffee?"

"I can't. I'm off to our Kathleen's. I was supposed to go yesterday when you called me over to yours. She'll be in a huff if I don't go today. I can't wait to tell her we've booked for Benidorm."

"Right, well I think I fancy a cup of overpriced coffee and a muffin. I'm going to Starbucks. See you tomorrow then. Let me know what your Kathleen's so desperate to see you about."

Feeling bright and cheerful again the pair went off in their opposite directions.

June walked the short distance up the street to the famous coffee shop, checked that it was not heaving with folk and stepped inside. Starbucks made a lovely cup of latte and even though she would not normally be prepared to pay the exorbitant prices, she felt in the mood to celebrate.

She spotted a table for two in the far corner of the coffee shop and plonked herself down. Her thoughts turned to the events of the past couple of days. Was this the day she finally got to wash her hands of Denis Goodman? She certainly hoped so and the thought of a week in the Spanish sunshine was really cheering her up even if her friend was threatening to go out on the pull in a thong. Yes, she decided, her life would be different from now on.

As June sipped her coffee, deep in thought, she didn`t notice someone had come to stand beside her. Then she heard a voice that took her out of her trance.

"June. June. Long time no see, as they say."

She looked up at the tall figure looking down on her, instantly recognising the voice.

"Nigel!" Standing by her side was her former husband.

"Got it in one. Can I join you?"

"Err...yes. You`re the last person I expected to see in here. It`s been years," she mumbled, unable to believe what she was seeing and hearing.

"I might say the same about you. Are you still living round her? I thought you might have moved on after...well you know what I mean."

"No, I`m still here. I have a flat in Chevins Road close to where I work." She wasn`t sure why she was being so free with her personal details but continued speaking, "What are you doing in these parts then Nigel? Didn`t you move to the Midlands with..."

Nigel finished her sentence for her, "Christine. Her name was Christine."

"Was?"

186

"Still is. But I haven't seen her for years. It didn't last long actually. Not once we moved away."

June was staring intently at Nigel. His hair was a little thinner on top but he still retained his natural light brown colouring with just a hint of grey around his temples. She couldn't help but notice he had a few laughter lines around his eyes. But they were still the loveliest blue eyes she had ever seen.

Nigel was carrying a few extra pounds around his middle and a hint of a double chin was obvious, but June thought the years had been kind to him.

"You look really well June. What have you been up to since I left? Sorry, it's none of my business. Forget I said that." Nigel's face was turning pink with embarrassment.

June saw how flushed he was looking and quickly changed the subject by asking, "Have you moved back to Burtley then or just passing through?"

"Neither. I'm an Area Manager now. Still working for the bank but I get to do a lot of travelling. I call up here every couple of weeks or so. I usually stay over at a Travel Lodge. I live alone so there's no one to rush home to."

June thought she detected a hint of sadness in his voice but decided to ask the obvious anyway.

"You haven't married again then?"

"No. Christine was up for it but I could never commit. She's a really nice woman but it was never love, not for me anyway."

Sipping her latte, which was now starting to go cold, June felt like pinching herself to make sure she was really having a conversation with her ex and not just dreaming. So many thoughts were swamping her brain. Why had their paths crossed today of all days? Was it fate or just a simple coincidence? What a day it was turning out to be.

"Can I get you another coffee? That one's gone cold with us talking. You haven't eaten your muffin either," Nigel asked.

June noticed that sat at a table across from them, a couple of old women were obviously eavesdropping on their conversation. For their benefit she spoke a little louder.

"Are you in a hurry to get off? My place is close so we could go back and have a more private chat without anyone earwigging."

The two old women took her hint and looked away.

Nigel was obviously not expecting June's offer but seemed happy to accept.

"I'm in no hurry. Like I said, I have no one to rush back to. So yes I'll be happy to go."

The couple stood up and pushed back their chairs, scraping them across the floor. Nigel, ever the gentleman, waited for June to go before him as they walked away from their table. The nosy old women were pretending not to notice what was happening. Out of sheer devilment June turned her head towards them and stuck out her tongue as she passed their table.

For the duration of the short walk to June's flat, both made idle chit chat about the weather, the amount of traffic passing through Burtley and how the town had changed over the years. June was finding herself feeling strangely at ease in Nigel's company, once the shock of seeing him again had subsided. Why she had invited him back had come as much of a surprise to her as it had to him. She had never been one for inviting guests back, with the exception of Maureen.

Nigel made himself comfortable on the sofa while June made coffee as promised. Whilst in her kitchen, waiting for the kettle to boil June was finding it much easier to talk to Nigel than she could ever remember. It was his kind and gentle nature that had attracted her to him in the first instance.

June carried their coffee mugs through to her living room and handed Nigel his. She sat herself down on the opposite end of the sofa, making sure she was keeping at least the width of a cushion between them for comfort.

He was the first to start a serious conversation. "Did you ever meet anyone special after we...parted?"

"No. I managed to find a job I actually do love and I've got a few good friends. Well one very close friend and a lot of work mates to keep me from being lonely. I'm fine. In fact I'd just booked a holiday only minutes before I went into Starbucks. I'm off to Benidorm with my best buddy, Maureen."

"Benidorm! Now I would not have had you down for Benidorm. Isn't it a little rowdy for you?" Denis seemed genuinely shocked at her choice of holiday destination.

"Well I'll soon find out. We go in a few weeks and what have I got to lose? Maureen has been, no she is a really good friend and I'm happy to go along with her choice. I owe her a lot."

"Now that's not the June I used to know. What's changed? There's something different about you but I can't quite put my finger on it."

"We live and learn Denis. Are you saying that you are still the same person that you were when we married? What have you learned about yourself as you've got older? I've learned an awful lot about myself and not all of it is good." June was finding words rolling off her tongue a little too easily and yet she was still feeling at ease baring her soul to Denis.

"Do you ever wonder how different things may have been for us if the miscarriage had never happened? I do. I would have liked to have been a parent. We would have been good parents," Nigel said wistfully.

"Mmm. It's crossed my mind many times. You would have been a wonderful father. I couldn't even do that for you either. I didn't do much at all when it comes down to it. I was so bitter about my own loss I didn't spare a thought about what you were feeling. I was totally selfish. Then I had my pills to numb everything and numb is all they did. I couldn't feel anything anymore. I got so used to feeling numb that I didn't want to stop feeling that way. I was too afraid of feeling and hurting again. When I did stop the pills it was all too late for us. We were strangers by then." June was still pouring her heart out and seemed unable to stop.

"I'd met Christine by then. I did try to understand and be sympathetic but there was no way I could break through the barriers you'd put up. Christine was just an escape from it all. She was available and I needed to escape at times. It was only ever sex that we shared. She didn't seem to be that bothered about me being

189

married at the time. I lived in hope that we could get ourselves sorted out and used Christine whenever I needed to. I`m not proud of what I did. After a while she started getting serious and you were so out of it I took the soft option and chose her. It was never going to last. I always knew that." Nigel`s words seemed to be full of regrets and apologies.

"Well, it`s all water under the bridge now. No amount of if`s and but`s will change anything. We both made mistakes and hopefully we`ll have managed to learn from them. It`s pointless going over it all again. We can`t turn the clock back." The tone of June`s voice signalled that she had obviously had enough of raking over the past. She steered their conversation towards work and started to explain what she was now doing to earn a living.

"I work in Field Hall Care Home now. I`ve been there ten years now and I really enjoy it. My friend Maureen, the one who I`m going to Benidorm with, she works with me. That`s how we met. So, things have worked out alright for me."

"Good. I`m glad you got sorted. I thought about you a lot. Wondering if you were coping." Nigel sounded sincere in what he was saying.

"The pay in this business isn`t very good but I had a small nest egg from my mother`s will, so I had enough to put down a bond on this flat and have a little put by for a rainy day as they say. You don`t have to worry about me anymore. I`m fine."

"I can see that you are. Well, it`s been really good seeing you June. You were the last person I expected to see today. Anyway, I`d better get my skates on or I`ll get stuck in rush hour traffic. My car`s back at the Travel Lodge."

Nigel stood up, stretched his arms and shoulders then set off walking towards the hall. June followed him, hardly able to believe what she was seeing. Never in a million years did she think she would see Nigel again. To have him come here to her home was inconceivable. But here he was and she was enjoying being in his company and he was going to walk out of her life once again.

As Nigel stepped outside into the communal hallway he turned around to take a last look at his ex-wife and smiled before saying,

"When I'm in the area again can we meet up and have a coffee? Only if you'd like of course, just as old friends."

June hesitated before replying, unsure of her feelings.

"Perhaps. I'll think about it. Let me have your mobile number."

Nigel took out his wallet and produced a business card then handed it over as he spoke.

"Take care June."

"You too."

She watched him turn away and start to walk towards the outer door. Seeing him walking away from her brought back the memory of the day they had parted. June had stood by the front door of their home on that day, watching him walk out of her life. He had turned around to take one last look at his wife then, just as he was doing today.

June had done nothing to stop him leaving then. *So why should I stop him going now,* she thought. She was too afraid to speak out back then but today she was supposed to be celebrating her freedom. A new start, a clean slate and a brighter future.

"Nigel! Nigel! Wait." The words were echoing down the hall before she had a chance to think about what she was saying. "Come back inside. I need to tell you something."

On hearing his name being called, Nigel turned around and started to walk back towards June, anxiously waiting by the door.

"What is it?" he said with genuine concern in his voice.

"Come back inside and close the door."

Looking a little confused, Nigel stepped back inside and closed the door behind him, then followed June back into her living room.

"Sit down and please don't ask any questions, just listen."

He perched on the seat cushion of the sofa and stared directly at her.

"Today has been a very special day for me. You turning up may have been just a coincidence, but I've got this gut feeling that it was meant to be. So, here goes." She drew in a very deep breath before she continued.

"I've been keeping a secret for forty years. If I had a pound for every time I wanted to tell you all about it, I would be rich. I was raped as a child."

Nigel's face turned white with shock.

"I was sexually abused on more than one occasion and eventually raped. I don't want to go into the nitty gritty because I want to put those memories behind me now. But, it's time you knew the real reason for me behaving the way I did towards you. I could never tell you back then because I felt ashamed. I'd kept it all a secret for so long I didn't know how or who to tell about it all."

Nigel just carried on staring at her.

"You're wondering who it was now. Well that's where my problems got so complicated. How do you tell your mother that her brother is a paedophile and better still, he chose his own niece to abuse? You know how my mother was about everything. You always said dust was never allowed to settle in her house. Well, how do you think she would have coped with a sack load of shit landing on her doorstep?

It started when I had piano lessons. My uncle Denis gave me lessons for free. When the funny business started I should have told my parents straight away but he scared me into keeping quiet. I'm not sure my mother would have believed it all. The sun shone out of his arse as far as she was concerned. He would have explained it all away as just being my imagination."

Nigel hadn't moved a muscle as he'd listened to June's revelations.

She continued, "Then he took things a stage further and I still didn't tell anyone. I finally refused to have any more lessons with him and still never told my parents why. Then he just announced he was moving away and that was the last we saw of him."

June paused and looked Nigel in the eyes. It was obvious he was at a loss for words.

"When I say it like this it all sounds so matter of fact. If it was someone else telling this to me I'd be asking why didn't they speak up in the first instance. If only it had been so simple. It's not just about feeling dirty and shameful, it's the power that they wield over their victim. He made me feel as if I was the guilty one. No one will ever understand unless they have been in that same situation, heaven help them."

Finally Nigel spoke, "I don't know what to say. It answers a lot of questions that I've asked myself over the years."

"Today is a new beginning for me. He's dead now and I've tied up a few loose ends today. There's no point in trying to analyse it all again, I've done all that and I just want to forget that man ever existed. I don't want to speak his name ever again. So, now you know it really wasn't anything that you did or didn't do Nigel. If we are to be friends then it all needed to come out today."

Nigel flopped back onto the sofa, never taking his eyes off of June. She returned his stare waiting for his response to her confession. It never came.

"Right, well that's given me something to be thinking about when I'm driving home," he finally commented. "I'm glad you found the courage to tell me."

It was obvious to him that June didn't want to discuss or divulge any more of her past. He stood up once again and started to make his way to the hall. June followed him to the door and opened it to let him out. As he brushed past her he stopped, turned to face her and said, "Call me sometime, when you're ready. Look after yourself June."

As he finished speaking he leaned over and kissed her gently on the cheek. June smiled back at him as he stepped outside.

"Drive carefully Nigel."

That evening, after a most memorable day, June retired to her bed feeling more relaxed than she could ever remember. Her thoughts turned to the events of the past twenty four hours. What a day it had turned out to be. She had so many questions that could not be answered. *Why today of all days had Nigel appeared back in her life? Was it some kind of sign from the powers that be, telling her everything was going to be fine from now on? Why had she felt the need to tell Nigel about her past? And when she had, how easy had it been to confide in him? Had she had found solace at last and put an end to her nightmares? Should she keep in touch with Nigel? Where would that lead them? What was her best friend going to make of it all? Was Maureen really going to wear a thong and go out on the pull in Benidorm?*

As she snuggled down under her duvet her thoughts turned to something she had done earlier in the evening. She had bought another interesting item from Amazon and was feeling quite excited about it. But she had one nagging thought about her purchase. *Would her new vibrator come complete with batteries?*

The End